9/09

A Democracy of Ghosts WITHDRAWN

A DEMOCRACY OF GHOSTS

A NOVEL BY JOHN GRISWOLD

La Grande, Oregon • 2009

© Copyright 2009, John Griswold
ISBN: 978-1-877655-63-0
Library of Congress Number: 2009920772

Publication Date: July 2009

Front Cover Art: October 1916 cover of *The Masses*, illustrated by Boardman Robinson, defaced by unknown library patron. Courtesy Special Collections, Michigan State University Libraries.

Title Page Photo: Funeral procession for Joe Pitkewicius (spellings vary), union miner killed in Herrin Massacre, 1922. Courtesy Gordon Pruett.

Back Page B/W Photo: "Shut This Door," Lewis Hine. Library of Congress, Prints & Photographs Division, National Child Labor Committee Collection, LC-DIG-nclc-01076.

Cover Design: Kristin Summers
(www.redbatdesign.com)
Text Design: David Memmott
Author Photo: Josh Birnbaum
(www.joshbirnbaum.com)

Published by
Wordcraft of Oregon, LLC
PO Box 3235
La Grande OR 97850

editor@wordcraftoforegon.com

Member of Council of Literary Magazines & Presses (CLMP)
and the Independent Book Publishers Association (IBPA)

Printed in the United States of America

FOR MY SONS

So many ghosts among us,
Invisible, yet strong,
Between me and thee, so many ghosts of the slain.

—D.H. Lawrence, "Erinnyes"

PROLOGUE

We call ourselves Little Egypt, and we were born to greatness; that was manifest. Steamboats once lined the wharves five-deep at Cairo, and Southern Illinois opened the first banks in the state when Chicago was just swamp and wild onions. The great Charles Dickens himself invested in us when it was pointed out how like Manhattan we were, bounded by two waterways greater than the Hudson and East Rivers, and for a short while we were the Ellis Island of the slavery and reconstruction South.

We felt in our souls the promise of destiny. Then Northern locomotives, fired with our coal and faster than any river barge, stole our future and shipped it away, blasting their horns in derision as they sped over the bridgespan we'd built for them. Mr. Dickens lost a bundle in that deal, and we hear he was none too happy, but after all it was our lives.

William J. Sneed was one of us. He pretended not to remember his origins, thinking it would keep him free, but he leaked parts of the story to us, his children's schoolteachers, the grocer, the honeywagon driver, other senators, mistresses and miners, and together we have known him well.

Willy Sneed was born the year the lake fell into the mines up at Braidwood and drowned all those men. Typhus killed his parents and left him in the state orphanage at the age of five. Two years later, when a new coal mine opened a mile north of Carterville, Billy was adopted by and bound to a practical miner and started as most of us did in that era, as a trapper boy. Monday through Saturday he never saw the sun. He rose before dawn, splashed his face with cold water, spooned beans from the evening meal into a dinner bucket and dripped blackstrap molasses over them then walked from his master's shack a few yards down a dirt road to the mine entrance, too tired to daydream of another place or time. Men and other boys crowded the rackety cage that descended again and again into the chambers 400 feet below.

Billy sat on a pile of gob behind a door made of scarred oak planks and opened it on demand of mule drivers pulling cars through the dark tunnels. Those teenage boys cursed and slapped him if he moved too slowly, and he had to close the enormous door again just as quickly to keep back the methane that naturally built up and exploded and killed us. He shared his spot and his lunch with the rats. He was lonesome for both his mothers, real and adoptive, and as a way of consoling himself he taught himself to read with the help of W.H. McGuffey and the glare of a carbide lamp.

In a few years Bill himself drove a mule pulling tons of soft coal through the tunnels. Muscles knotted on his calves, and veins stood out on his arms in blue strings. He had grown thinner as he got older, despite the miner's wife keeping food back from her husband to feed her children extra. Bill was confident, smart, a good-looking boy with droopy ears who would have been tall if he hadn't had to walk hunched all day, and he was liked in the mines and handy with young women in town. The miner's wife taught him what she could of the Bible, and he read everything else he found— union tracts, a copy of *Macbeth* left by a traveling carnival troupe, railway schedules, and the few books he bartered from the company dentist in exchange for working the treadle that powered the drill.

Despite his learning we expected him to stay in those dark, rumbling tunnels for the rest of his life, as we stayed, year after year, until we died from silicosis or were crippled beyond utility. Bill would become his master's laborer, like an apprentice tending a craftsman, and pick up the slabs of felled coal and heave them into the carts. When he became a man he would be given his own section of the face to hack at and his own laborer, who would have grown up underground too. If he was lucky, and some were, he might work the mines sixty years or more. It was a hard life that made us hard people, but we fist-fought each other in the bars, union halls and employment offices for the right to dig, lay track, blast, brattice and brace.

Around that time there were two dozen soft coal mines in our Egypt. Outsiders owned them, along with our quarries, orchards, and factories, while we did all the work. It's true, those men had acumen and gumption, and somebody had to front the money to get things rolling, but since we did not own the means of our lives, we pointed to The Book's first dictum and asked, "Is this not the basis for a Christian capitalism?"

Too thin and growing homely, Will Sneed was elected, on the basis of one impromptu speech he made to us at a rally, to his first political office, local union financial secretary. He ran unopposed. In addition to his full-time job undercutting the coal face and his minor bookkeeping, he somehow found the time to speak to us about labor issues. He was rough as a cob and dumb as a bear cub, but he amused us, so we applauded his speeches that were based on words of better socialists than him. He was limited, you see, because he came from us. He had no parents, was neither a landowner nor a pioneer name, and we realized despite popular stories to the contrary that even American will and imagination had its limits.

John Mitchell talked to the young man one cold morning with crocuses sprouting from the slag heaps and the smell of wet earth in the air. This was just into the new century, and Mitchell, union figurehead, revered to the point of being hung with the saints on miners' walls, knew a leader when he saw one and praised Will for our solidarity in the struggle against those who would challenge the rights of free working men. Will had so much energy afterward he worked an extra half-shift without pay.

Will met Cora Stallons in 1904. Her daddy was a shopkeeper in the next town over who owned his own Stutz. Will had had a sister named Cora whom he had not seen since he was sent to the orphanage, and Cora Stallons liked Will's English surname better than that of the Italian boy trying to court her. Two months later they were married under an arbor of climbing roses in Cora's father's backyard, and in no less than nine months, along came their first child, Ruby, dark and curly as a gypsy with a mole on her cheek and the character to match, and as soon as Will's pants hit the bedpost again, there was Carl, image of his daddy, but with an easier row to hoe.

By the time the Great War blew up like a wicked rumor, William and Cora had three children and a fourteen-year marriage. They still lived in one of our little coal towns, but William had managed an education of sorts and was different from himself now and even further from us. He said he was a Jeffersonian Republican of the McKinley bent, and he read Paine, Emerson, Carlyle and the Muhlbach tales for relaxation. By his charisma and his confidence that we would believe in his new version of things, we did.

He studied further and hung out his shingle, and we began to hope we might produce our own downstate Lincoln, even though a few of us still threw parties on the anniversary of the original's murder. William's practice flourished, and he forged political allies yet stayed in touch with the rank and file of miners, able and proud to say, "I am formed from the same as they."

We were as irreducible as carbon, as full of energy as the coal we dug and breathed. We needed to show the rest of the state that we weren't suckers any more so we elected William J. Sneed, Jr., to the state senate in 1920, the year his last child was born, to return something to the common good. For a decade Sneed would represent us in the state legislature and protect us from northern butchers with broad shoulders, a task more important to us than federal matters anyway.

We loved Mr. Sneed all the more now that his humble past was past and congratulated ourselves that we'd supported him from the very first. We built a brick foursquare for his family and watched him furnish it with a multitude of books, mica lamps, leather armchairs with leather footstools, and the first electric icebox in town. He deserved a nice home because he was an educated man, polite in conversation, strong in negotiation, and calm in conflagration. We also voted him President of United Mine Workers Association Sub-District 12 of District 12, heart of the most radical community in America of its time.

Radical or not, some of us wanted it all ourselves—the Turkish stair-runner, meat on the table every day of the week, the privy in the house, the smiles and nods of our neighbors. Sneed never had nothing 'til we sent him up, not a pot to piss in nor a window to throw it out of, and now we guess he had a pretty good thing while we didn't even own automobiles, and sometimes he'd talk to people he knew all his life and sometimes no. Even his wife was a little distant-turned.

We were a family and that's no apology. We ate supper then sat on the porch to watch the pulse of fireflies in the deepening dark, the kids up the oaks at the side of the house and music coming from the new cabinet radio. This was the deep contentment of human life, what might be gained from a life examined, planned and executed, not at all a settling-for until some vindication by a glowering, gloating god.

Yet dangers surrounded us: reds, addicts, vintners, godless, dries, fascists, Johnny-Come-Latelies, Papists, lawless rogues, and Protestant preachers who taught civic duty. Each was a stone in the pond with concentric rings widening into a possible future, and when the rings intersected, the water grew confused. The people wanted peace, desperately, but someone had to mine the coal; to stand for fair pay and dignity; to grade the road to everlasting life with exemplary moral conduct; and to share wine at table with three generations just as it had been done in Lombardy. Our rights, as we saw them, included life, liberty, certitude, work stoppages to create artificial demand, gambling away the balance of our Friday pay on Saturday night, and the pursuit of Romero's daughter, if she'd have us. In the absence of several of these things we were forced to try to reshape the world in our own images.

Senator Sneed assured us that our sulfur coal and civic unity would usher in a new age of brotherhood and prosperity, that the crops in our stony fields would flourish and find markets, and that our children would never war again. He explained to us the massacres of our brothers and sisters by that rascal king Rockefeller, and the rhetoric of our new hero, John L. Lewis, who would say, "The public does not know that a man who works in a coal mine is not afraid of anything except his God; that he is not

13

afraid of injunctions, or politicians, or threats, or denunciations, or verbal castigations, or slander—that he does not fear death."

But we *were* frightened, and exhilarated, and we wanted the world another way, without revolution, turmoil or more pain. We had had enough pain to go around.

In the exhaustion of those few years after the war, we knew only that we *wanted*. And William J. Sneed did his best to represent us all in these disparate and discordant desires.

CHAPTER ONE

James O'Rourke hadn't meant to be a scab, not the type that got killed. He was an American and angry because nothing was ever simple.

He woke curled on the seat just as they pulled in, his limp fingers through the handle of his cardboard suitcase. He got dizzy when the conductor again yelled, "Carbondale this stop Carbondale." O'Rourke had known of another Carbondale in the East and a woman who had talked over some dinner—Father fuels in Pennsylvania before his long haul to Jacksonville poor dear—and now O'Rourke was on a train and didn't know the time.

It was midnight. His body remembered itself first, reminded by fatigue, the gritty sweat of travel on his face and the rumple of his pants digging into him painfully. He was very sensitive and couldn't seem to get comfortable anywhere.

The platform was dark and in the dark lot outside the terminal the beams of an idling dump truck pointed unevenly at nothing. He had never been so close to such large machinery, and there was something sublime in its scale, in the thrum and rumble of its huge engine, in the acrid fumes that smelled like work, but he bravely pulled himself on to the running board by the long mirror that jutted from the cab like a big ear. The driver jerked his thumb at the bed of the truck and turned away to smoke his cigarette. O'Rourke was too exhausted to be anything but peeved. He was an administrator, not some dirty coal digger, and he deserved more courtesy than that. At least, he thought, I won't have to talk to the driver, you reuben you.

Wooden ribs held canvas over the bed of the truck, conestoga-fashion. O'Rourke swung a leg high over the tailgate and, pulling himself up, found benches on both sides and fuzzy shadows sitting on them, staring back in pale disapproval. He sat by the tailgate, next to one of the formless men. The heat from the man's leg on his own came as a shock and broke the spell.

"Fellas," O'Rourke said and nodded in the dark.

Still no one spoke; it was very rude, even terrifying. The man next to him held a bolt-action rifle upright between his knees.

They began, pulling alone onto an empty state highway. Once they got up to speed, the chill summer air whipped a corner of wet canvas against the back of O'Rourke's head again and again. The engine roared monotonously, never rising or falling in pitch, and the truck yawed rhythmically on its heavy springs. No one in the bed spoke or even seemed to be awake, lying with heads back against the wooden slats or foreheads down on the muzzles of their rifles, like a cargo of suicides. Occasionally the tires hit large potholes, and some of the men stirred and tried to wrap jackets more tightly around themselves or shifted their weight on the bench planks. O'Rourke shivered and checked his pocket watch every few minutes.

After an hour the truck slowed, turned and jolted along a high-crowned dirt road. O'Rourke held himself off the seat with his clenched fists, sure he was being bruised. He practiced in his head the ultimatum he would deliver the mine manager when they finally met: You'd best not take for granted at *all* that just because I'm here I'm staying. And if I leave, and chances are damned good I do—this abuse is *ridiculous*—someone is going to drive me in a proper automobile to a good hotel before I get put on a train tomorrow back to Chicago at *your* expense.

Brakes squealed metal-on-metal, and O'Rourke was thrown against his neighbor. He thought the man might actually have shoved him back with his shoulder. Someone outside shouted unintelligibly over the noise, and the driver shut down the engine. O'Rourke's ears rang with the complete silence, and his back and legs tingled. No one else moved, so O'Rourke jumped out of the truck, landing with one hand still tightly grasping the steel tailgate, like a swimmer gone overboard. The men in the truck stayed put, and O'Rourke could hear them in there, breathing in the dark.

More ghosts emerged from the night and began climbing in over the tailgate by twos. O'Rourke panicked; maybe he'd been mistaken in thinking they had arrived. He was slow to get back in because he was afraid to push, and the only place left to sit was the cold steel floor. Legs of men rose around him, reminding him of being a child trapped in a crowd of adults. He leaned out when the truck rumbled to life and saw by the headlights the derricks and rail cars and out-buildings, the big and small mounds of coal, the mutilated earth. He had never seen a mine before, but surely this was what one looked like, and how many could there be?

Within minutes they came to a town. O'Rourke knelt again, getting dirty looks from the men closest to him, and evaluated it professionally as they drove through. Two hotels, a telegraph office, a bank, an unusual number of churches. Bronze doughboy in the middle of a small square. Trolley tracks through the dirt, leafy side streets with wooden sidewalks and a few gas lamps. Lots of Sear bungalows and brownstones. Quaint, quiet and deadly, O'Rourke decided, nothing at all like his idea of a company town.

Sitting down painfully he jostled the man next to him, who shocked him by smiling into his face at close range. The man shouted over the engine and rattling metal that his name was Antonio Malkovaich. O'Rourke shouted, "What's this?" and pointed to the last houses on the outskirts of town.

"Herrin," Malkovaich said.

"What's going on here?" O'Rourke said.

"Nothing goes on in Herrin," Malkovaich said, missing the point. "There's sometimes something happening in Marion. Doesn't matter, though. It's generally too hot to walk to either one in the daytime, and it's not safe to go out at night."

"But it's safe now?"

Malkovaich laughed and backhanded O'Rourke's chest playfully.

O'Rourke flinched as if he'd been struck much harder and let the matter drop. They turned onto a larger state road, raced along with the knobbed tires whining on the blacktop, and after a few minutes reached a hamlet set in four corners of a crossing.

"This is it," Malkovaich said. He motioned O'Rourke out of the truck as the guards pressed forward, bent double under the tarp, and when O'Rourke looked at him, Malkovaich waved more urgently.

A general store with a tall false front, something out of that Cisco

17

Kid western, slouched against two roadhouses squatting in the dark like crypts. A third tavern, across the dirt road, had newspaper pasted over its windows, but light leaked through them and under the door, and blades of light shined between gaps in the bead-and-board siding. No-account shacks backed the tavern in a semicircle and faded into the dark.

"What is it?" O'Rourke asked, keeping Malkovaich close.

"Pistol City. Real name is Colp. So wet you have to wring out your clothes when you leave. Gambling, women. Snow. Whatever you want. Used to be colored-only, now some white trash too."

"So we're safe here?" O'Rourke said.

"What do they care you're a scab, long as you pay," Malkovaich said. He shrugged. "They don't care. Not much, I guess."

"Scab?" O'Rourke said.

They entered Ma Hatchett's through a side door. The bartender woke an old man asleep in a chair against the wall, and he returned with six women still pulling their work clothes on. The older women rubbed their eyes as if they had been woken, but some of the younger girls were drunk and knocked against the armed men, tried to take their rifles and made insulting comments they pretended were in jest. A piano player sat down with a drink and began to bang out a popular German tune from the war, but two of the guards went and stood over him so he switched to "The Rose of No Man's Land."

Despite the strangers, the guns, the dark primitive country, O'Rourke felt he understood this place even beyond the familiarity of a barroom. With liquor in hand and under the comforting gaze of women, he relaxed and let his memory of the guards' bizarre silence in the truck change in his mind to something less sinister. After all he had no experience with the world of rural workers, miners—coal miners—and his unease was probably mistaken. Now he thought of their quiet solidarity as that of a longtime marriage, which he imagined as having the dignity of well-oiled furniture.

The guards livened up after a few drinks too, and O'Rourke began to joke around. Not with them, but with another of the unarmed men, who said he was a mechanic and a poker player. O'Rourke liked him for the way his manner changed when O'Rourke introduced himself as a mine executive. The kid was stupid as a carp, O'Rourke saw, but his deference showed good manners. O'Rourke regally accepted the mechanic's admiring glances and stood, back to the bar, glass to chin, surveying the room.

It was loud and warm, and the Pinkertons had another round and talked about women in general as they held these particular women in their laps. O'Rourke watched from the side and thought with a tickle of pleasure in his stomach that it was too bad Pistol City wasn't closer to Chicago. Imagine Old Man Haskel and his thugs coming in a place like this to try to take O'Rourke out from under the protection of his own men. Why, he'd!

The men drank to get drunk with an abandonment that suggested a deadline, shouting in celebration when a Pink fell against the bar and the bottles shivered in the din. O'Rourke's vision spun in the light from bare bulbs hanging by their wires and coal oil lamps flaming orange inside chimneys smoked black. He considered his glass, poor Yorick, and wondered if it was wood alcohol. Something sure didn't feel right. Busthead came from bad distillation, he thought scientifically, but how? Was it an accident with a proper still or did you have to build it wrong in the first place?

Men sneered and waved dollar bills, and the women's lips peeled back as they shouted obscenities in the men's ears. Children stood in the back door, some in diapers, others old enough to have an interest in bare flesh. O'Rourke thought of that old joke he couldn't remember. Fitting, whatever it was. Oh, yes: the orphanage in the valley between the nunnery and the monastery. One of the dirt babies reached for a glass of beer on a table and a woman slapped his hand away and everyone burst into laughter.

The last thing O'Rourke remembered clearly was a whore pulling her dress down to her waist and wrapping both meaty hands around an engorged breast. She squeezed hard, like she was strangling a chicken, and squirted milk five feet across a table into a gunman's eye. The saloon exploded in hilarity.

When O'Rourke woke, he knew he'd been unlucky. If the mines had been running, the girl would have had him in and out and stepping lively. The way it was, beds were no longer a commodity. If johns wanted to roll over and fall asleep on a lousy mattress, that was their business, so long as they woke up thirsty, hungry, horny or all three.

O'Rourke sat on the edge of the pallet that lay on the floor. The piano was butchering a rag in the next room. He hadn't slept long, and the hangover was just beginning, surfacing from the remains of the drunk like the jagged spars of some wreck in Lake Michigan. Oh yeah, he'd be sick, he knew, only a matter of when. Oh god. Oh my god, he thought. Let's go. You can do it. Whores spoke calmly, bored, nearby. Their indifference made it worse, but the piano was the worst since it played sharp. He stood stiffly and pushed aside the yellowed sheet that served as a door.

A few scabs still leaned on the bar, too drunk to look up at him. The girl said she didn't take his wallet. He said he had his wallet, it was right here, but everything in it was gone. She asked what was in it. Cash, he said, you smartass little bitch. Receipts he needed to be reimbursed, a gold toothpick in a leather slipcase, and his only photograph of his girl. Mercy, he said, thinking that giving them her name might make them sympathetic. The older women laughed, and the young whore sat very still while they teased him and asked if Mercy knew what a dirty bird he was.

O'Rourke tried to get city-wise again. The girl with whom he had just shared his intimacy punched him in the gut and walked away. He wasn't ready for it, and she hurt him bad. That can kill a guy, he thought, as the girl called for Ma somewhere in the back. Even through the pain, it was interesting to him that there was a Ma Hatchett; so often there wasn't.

Outside he rose from the cool earth and climbed into the truck to lie on a bench until the other men came. He thought the cold air on the drive back would help, but the jouncing and exhaust fumes gave him a migraine instead, and by the time they got to the mine he believed he was as sick as he had ever been in his life. The others pushed him out; those with weapons slung them on their shoulders and filed into the darkness. Someone else beckoned with a crooked finger and led him by flat moonlight to a boxcar on a siding. It might have been the devil himself, for all O'Rourke knew; he had enough life left in him to feel despair.

O'Rourke pulled himself into the rail car with great difficulty. He'd never been in one, and it surprised him how uncomfortable its cold edges and splintered wooden floor were. His wingtips encountered cabinets and boxes, and he fell forward on a desk before he found the cot next to it with both his hands held far out, blindly. He collapsed on it, fully dressed. There was no blanket, and he was shivering so hard that it made his head worse, like he'd been speared through one eye and out the top of his skull. He crawled to the open door to vomit.

Mosquitoes whined, but he couldn't battle them. As they bit his weak flesh, he felt the earth spin, even the railcar in on the conspiracy, and never having known such a sorry place ever existed on all of God's green earth, and asking why me, and how long, he was absolved in his misery and helplessness by passing out into dead sickly sleep.

CHAPTER TWO

Steam rose from the joint between the tun funnel and condensing coil. Sally made a quick paste of flour and water and smeared it on the pinhole, where it cooked instantly and held. She stoked the small oak fire—coal was plentiful but could scorch the mash if it wasn't watched—and changed the Ball jar that caught the liquor. She left the lean-to and returned to the one-room house she and Bullyrag had built.

She felt as if he had come suddenly into the room; he had not. Bullyrag tied her to Crenshaw Crossing, his bulk and presence, his walk and weight, and she felt lightheaded, able to see but not to comprehend when he was gone, a blindness identical to rage that saw the world but couldn't take it in.

She wiped her hands on the front of her shirt then dug deep in a pine box in a corner of the room, felt under the covers and the bolt of linen inside, and came up with the journal. She dated the page June 16 and after long thought wrote, "Two pints. B working. Mines still out. Day is fine."

Bully was helping Jake Drummond on his tiny farm. Drummond might even pay in pork. Sally carried the journal to the kitchen table, cut a slice of bread and chewed it slowly, respectful of the earth and its things. She read the short entry above the one she had started.

"May. Raining again. Jacob has died. Remember his chin, nose. Eyes. Flattened hair."

The words no longer brought him back the way she wanted, and she wished again there had been a photograph made.

Would it have mattered? That awe-ful disconnect of the photograph, the phonograph, the movies, each of them saying, "Here's the thing so important to you, keep up your pretense that anything lasts." The new technologies were imperial: "Make do with what you have, this scrap of paper or celluloid, it's good enough for the likes of you." And one clearly saw the emptiness behind that meager presence, the person so completely not-there that one fell into a swoon in time.

She remembered, against her will, the difficulty of removing dirt trapped under her nails after planting tulip bulbs on the grave. Crows in the trees squawking at some tabby cat trying to hide in the grass. Before that, the blast of wet wind as Bullyrag on hands and knees, soaked, head down, dug fast, angrily, hit the remains of some animal but didn't slow, didn't seem aware he was tossing bones out with the dirt. Under them there was pea coal and then a solid vein, and when he stood up and got the pick and hunched again over the hole, it frightened her to see how brutally he could swing.

Then she'd put Jacob in swaddling cloth in that square black coffin of coal with some Tiger Lilies she picked. The First Baptist preacher showed up only as Bully was covering the grave back over and said a few words about little children and the kingdom of heaven, but Sally thought of *Chronicles* instead: "For we are strangers before thee, and sojourners, as were all our fathers: our days on the earth are as a shadow, and there is none abiding." She knew that once something went down into the earth, it was lost forever.

Now she began to feel angry with herself for forgetting the main thing. She checked on Robert, asleep in a box and breathing easily. Poor little Robert in her arms, watching his brother get buried. But he's too young to remember, she thought, and forgetting is a blessing from God.

Robert no longer looked like Jacob had, or like an infant at all, sprouting new length, baby fat gone. He had lived to remind them of their loss. All she ever wanted was her babies, always.

Sally chewed her bread and forced the anger down by continuing the proper line of thought. Soil curled under the plow, seed was spread downwind by handfuls from a bag, grain reaped. Just like that, the seasons pass, a time for everything under the sun. Threshing the wheat to separate the chaff; stone-grinding the flour and mixing it with pure cold water, salt, and yeast; kneading the dough, waiting for its rise and punching it back, resting, rising, falling. Sacrificing it to the fires of the oven. And all that joyful gladdening toil to take Him in my mouth in remembrance,

23

remembering him in my mouths and the multitude of joy, brawls, tears, tenderness. A great house of humanity.

Sally couldn't think of anything to write so she put the journal away under everything else in the box and swept the house clean of the gray dust that threatened to bury them. Six houses stood at the Crossroads. Billy, she was sure, would stop on his return. Much to do these days. People thought you could relax when the mines were down. She wanted to keep the house for Bullyrag, especially after his accident, and Jacob's death. She didn't mind scrubbing floors—that kind of work was where a large part of her strength came from—but the dust filtering down slowly and endlessly was maddening.

Jacob had been colicky that afternoon, Bully said, and he stopped crying after Sally got home. That was all, really. In three hours he was dead. The midwife protested that she had done her part at the delivery; when called she stood uselessly and watched him die.

Sometimes there's reasons for these things, Sally thought.

She felt an enormous rage and oppression in the shack. She closed her eyes and felt herself standing on a treeless plain with a cast-iron sky pressing down from above, about to crush her. She realized she was picturing the inside of a mine.

Soup to simmer for the families, flowers to pick, whiskey to sell, and always, political action. To organize: the infinitive of life. Coercion, wheedling, subtle hints of threat at the mention of her husband's force. Women do so much.

She had learned a lot at the coking ovens in Pennsylvania, where she worked side-by-side with Bullyrag as he lifted and shoveled tons of the rock each day and pulled the carts like a draft horse. She got to know him really for the first time, after two years of marriage, by watching him work. She shoveled coal into the ovens and pulled coke from them in glowing heaps, madly, rapidly, trying to keep up with Bullyrag but unable to, and then understanding at a glance that she was not being tested—he wouldn't even think of it—which only made her love him more and work harder than ever. There she had learned she could work as hard as a man, the strongest man she had ever known, yes, she could, given separate tasks. Together they made a lot of money. And though there were train tickets to be bought to come back west, hotels, picture shows and good dinners with wine at the European Hotel in Herrin, what was left bought them the materials for their house, which Bully built, with her help, and they had been free and clear.

Sally had a great wide back and took pride that she was known for both her strength and her temper. People listened when she talked. She had organized those women out East to march over the ridges. She took them mine to mine, stood at the beginning of each shift at each mine and spoke of brotherhood. And the men who had never considered them in this light were surprised when they found them not laughable but sensible, and she watched it flit across their faces as doubt and then determination.

The men forgot them then and thought the idea had been their own, and they struck, one mine after the next. And it was Sally, while Bullyrag was still finding men to follow him, who took the women back to their rightful houses on company land, where they had lived when they worked the mine and had been evicted when the scabs were brought in. Sally led them in the charge, threw scalding water on the new women through the windows they used to clean. They beat the scab wives with ax handles, ripped their dresses, and after they ran out, broke their wooden spoons and bowls, pissed on their bedclothes and threw them out through the same windows. Finally the strangers, standing horrified at the edge of camp, caved and fled as a group into the woods as if Sally and her group were a disaster or a visitation, and by God they were. She sure was.

Sneed's car pulled into the yard under a maple. The children of The Crossing ran out to greet him. He wore a flat straw boater, braces, wire glasses that made him look more frail and, to Sally's eyes, older than he was. He had lost most of his hair. Sally worried for him. He was wearing away faster than Bullyrag, and Sneed didn't labor. Sally wondered if she would be dry and thin too, old before her time, if she had been educated. Cora had best take care of him. Sally didn't like the way she argued with him.

He gave out hard candies to the children and shook Otis Clark's hand.

"Yes, just came from there, and the situation is tense, but I don't expect trouble," he said to more men who came from their shacks to get the news. "Certain violations of the law. Definitely a nonunion proposition."

She remembered the two of them under the table, tickling the adults' feet and stifling giggles behind the Irish lace tablecloth hanging down to hide them from grownup eyes. Then Billy went to work the mine, and he was no longer a boy, never mind his age. But a man could learn a craft then, and Father was one of the best, the Welsh always were. Cared for the family so they never went wanting. Incredible that in those days they decided when and how much to work, and if you needed extra cash you worked some more. Then the machines and their managers came, and now it was unimaginable to think there was a time when men and women controlled their own wages, which is to say, their own lives.

The wives of Crenshaw came out after the men, with more children, twenty people or more, and Sneed greeted most of them by name before he walked up on Sally's porch and kissed her. They went inside.

She poured a little whisky in the one china cup she owned, and Sneed sipped it delicately with his big hand grasping the top of the cup.

"Sally, you've done so much already," he said.

Listen here, she thought testily: When Bullyrag lost his two best fingers and thumb on his right hand—the holy trinity we called them after they were gone and he was left with no sensation in the others to feel what he was doing, so our lovemaking had to change—and I went below with him in the night to the darker night of the shaft and then the tunnels, terrified for never having been there before but laughing out loud when he called the rooms breasts. It's their name he said and laughed, but yours are better, better than Mother Earth's herself. Firing all the charges at once after the men had gone home. Sitting together in silence waiting for hangfires, Bullyrag gently stroking the stumps of the fingers he'd lost just days earlier from a charge he thought the fuse went out on. What did it feel like? she'd asked him. Like a hard slap, he said. Giving or receiving? she asked. He grinned then and said, Just shows you ain't given nor had enough to know. We went back into the rooms to make sure all the charges had blown as they should, knowing a lot worse could happen than losing a couple of fingers. Yes, I've done my part, you insolent bastard. Dear brother.

"Rest assured, Sally, I'm doing everything I can," Sneed said.

"I believe we need to get the men together and tell them."

"I'm a believer in the capacity for self-realization through reason," he said and grinned from one side of his mouth. "Yet neither to affirm nor to deny the existence of anything until proven by trial."

"Don't be showing off. Do you want to hear or not?"

"Tell me about your second sight, then. You and Mother," he said.

Sally's anger came up fast but subsided when she saw him grin and adopt the appropriate look of interest.

"We were talking out back after a meeting. A week ago to the day. A dozen of us from here plus those men from Hardin County. The Meneese girl said something, and I asked her what, but she wouldn't say it again, so I came in to check on Robert. When I looked on the curtain on that east window, there was an angel on it. She was holding my poor dead Jacob. Her hair flowed down over my baby like a blanket, and the sweetest smile played on her lips. But she was strong, Billy, and I knew not to go near, that the child belonged to her now. We all stayed that way a full minute, me in the doorway with the neighbors behind looking in, and the angel with Jacob in her arms wavering as the curtain blew with the breeze. She grew fainter and fainter until she was just gone. Those farthest in the back asked me what it was, and I told them an angel had come for my baby's soul. That started the younger kids bawling, and their mothers got spooked and ran out with them hanging on their skirts. Bully says he didn't see anything, but…. I did, Billy. At the time I took some comfort that my baby was with Jesus and wouldn't ever face the wicked ways of this world again."

And that was only one baby, Sally thought; I still have my other baby, who I'll feed and watch grow up a man to do great things beyond Bully or Billy or any of these men.

"Thing is, Billy, I was wrong," Sally said. "My baby didn't die for no good reason. The angel came to warn us through him."

"Bully's a good hardworking man," Sneed said. He couldn't stop himself from glancing at the wall where the dying Christ hung on a foot-long black crucifix hand-carved from coal. It hung near the angel's window. "And you need to think more of your family now and less of union matters. Keep Bully away from that mine, Sally. Present and accounted for, and no trouble. Are you listening to me? There's more efficacious ways to do these things, so leave it to those you elected to do their jobs."

"Please, Billy, I saw them right there."

"Okay, Sally," Sneed said. He didn't look again, just in case. "I'll stress the dangers even more than I have."

"Someone's going to die, Billy."

"No one will die. Leave it to us. Where's Bully now?"

"Drummond's."

"Good. I'm glad Drummond hired him on after all. Keep him near to you. We were at that mine this morning. I didn't poke too deeply, but I saw rifles, and a whole pile of ammunition under some open books, and what might have been a Gatling under a tarp. Several of the buildings were locked, and we didn't talk about opening them up."

He smiled. "Thaxton, his deputies, and the National Guard commander went with me. Pegleg McDowell's scabs know they're headed for trouble. One of them tried to blend in with my group, and Thaxton pointed him out to me. It'd be easier in the short run to let them run away a few at a time, but I can't afford to do them favors. The next ones Lester hires will be even more desperate for work, and Lester'll use more guards, and maybe they'll manage to crush us this time."

"Lester can't last as long as us."

"He has deep pockets. Even now he's arranging for more capital from a group in Indiana to see him through."

Sally asked, "What'd you say to that scab that was trying to run?"

"I pretended not to see him and whispered a word to Pegleg. He walked back to his office and called the man's name out loudly as if he was surprised not to find him there already. The poor fellow looked like he wanted to cry, and I told Wallace to get between him and me so I could get in the car."

"Yes, poor fellow," Sally said dryly. "Stealing food from my baby's mouth. They'll all get what they deserve in the next life."

"Sally, if there's...."

"I know, if we do, I'll ask. Bully's proud, though. He made me send back those clothes. Besides, we're doing good, see for yourself."

Sneed didn't look around the single room. "Tomorrow morning's the meeting at Sunnyside. Remind Bully I asked him to be there," he said. "And let me know if you need anything."

He's sincere even if he is a politician, Sally thought. And he's always favored me over the others. Still love him for that. Strange how the feelings are deeper than for my blood brothers. More complicated. But raised together after all. He is me if I had been a man, maybe. As smart? My looks going too. Bully.

Bullyrag Greathouse walked toward them as a flatbed truck pulled away from the crossroads. He had a deliberate, far-reaching walk that made it seem he wore seven-league boots. Sally ran out, kissed him, wrapped one leg around behind his knee. He grabbed her and squeezed her ass with his good hand. He was still sweating, and straw was caught in his dusty hair.

"Top of the morning, Senator," Bullyrag said with a grin.

"Mr. Greathouse," Sneed said. He offered his hand and the other man clasped and shook it warmly.

Sally noted he took Bully's damaged hand in his own. Most didn't.

"Meeting tomorrow," Sneed said. "Hope to see you there. The men rely on you. So do I."

"I'll be there. You have a good afternoon now, and see you don't charge those kids more than a quarter to peek at the inside of your limousine," he said. "That's the taxpayers' car."

"It would've been cheap at twice the price," Sneed said. "Maybe you want to take your piece of it now, Bully. I could spare the hood ornament and no harm done."

The Lincoln's back door was open, and Wallace Duncan, Sneed's son-in-law, driver, and an Illinois State Trooper, helped kids out of the backseat.

Sally watched the Lincoln disappear at the head of a phalanx of dust that boiled up then settled on The Crossing. She'd have to sweep again. While Bully washed up from a pail in the yard, Sally sneaked the journal out from the bottom of the pine box and added to it.

"Billy here at noontime. Bully is back."

Finished with the day's entries, she put the journal away. Just summer is all, she thought, the smell of honeysuckle and wet ferns in the shade under the poplars. Lying under a tin roof in the unsleepable heat next to the one I love and follow, my brother-in-arms, both soldiers in the struggle for life, covered in sweat and sex and the dust of Egypt. And more children will follow, sure as rivers run to the sea. There'll be more of us all one day.

CHAPTER THREE

Sneed walked easily down Park Avenue, keeping under the awnings, waving to men loading their Fords parked at a slant to the curb. Some of them were farmers, some miners, and some did a little of both, but everyone knew who he was. He moved with an athletic grace in his boxy shoes, and, feeling good, he hollered to Martin Zwick, rolling down the awning in front of his clothing store, loudly enough to be heard over the trolley that rang its bell as it approached the stop at the European Hotel. Sneed turned right on Ninth, tipped his hat to a woman from church, and hurried on to the Western Union. The inside of the building was damp and cool and smelled of hair tonic and talcum that seeped through the connecting door to the barbershop. One of the men who'd been hanging around the union headquarters yesterday and now was loafing in the barbershop—Tom Radovich from Number Nine, an undercutter Sneed remembered by his accent—saw him through the barbershop window and hurried out. He shook Sneed's hand with both of his own.

"It's right what you say, Mr. Sneed," he said. "I believe it too. My wife too, she says we stick it out to the end."

"Fine, Tom. Be sure you pick up your rations at the union hall tomorrow. Plenty for everyone. Children okay, Tom?" He didn't know if the man had children or not.

"Yes, thank you, Mr. Sneed. My littlest girl? Her teeth? Yes, teeth come in, and we tell her she looks like wolf. Wolf to eat up those scabs!"

Sneed laughed harder than needed, and he saw that it confused Radovich, who wasn't making a joke. "Good day, Tom," he said, feeling suddenly tired.

"I wish you good day too, sir."

Sneed stepped lightly through the front of Bailey's newsstand, two aisles filled with children's toys and barrels of hard candy. He nodded to Bailey, who was talking on the phone, and waited with Hal Trovillion among stacks of the *St. Louis Globe Democrat*, the *Chicago Tribune*, and several local papers.

"Morning, Curly," Hal said.

Sneed had only a wreath of fine hair around the back of his head. He smiled.

"Hi, Three-Piece. Any news fit to print?"

"I'd like to report on the big meeting out at Sunnyside in the morning. At least I hear there's a big meeting," Trovillion said. "Think I'll be allowed into this one?"

Sneed picked up a copy of the *Herrin News* as if it was unclean. "If you don't make it to the meeting, what will you fill this with?"

"There's always news. Ida Triplett claims her husband wasn't fully dead when they buried him and wants him dug back up. Coroner told her he'd seen dead before, and Triplett was *dead*, and if he wasn't before, he is now. She says when they dig him up they'll find his poor fingers scratched to the bone from trying to claw out of the casket. I guess the beatings she took from that old man weren't enough for one life. She must want him back for more."

"Maybe she hates the idea of him getting away without getting her licks in. Cora always said Ida should have waited until he was sleeping it off one afternoon and then hit him in the head with a good solid Griswold skillet. It's enlightening."

"Drowning was good enough for him in the end. Too bad he was too drunk to appreciate the experience. They say he left the widow a fine fishing rod." Trovillion pretended to sort change and said casually, "Your goons kept me from going out with you this morning."

Sneed looked over the top of his glasses. "I didn't tell any men to do that, Hal. Seriously. We're not fascists."

"Not reds, either, but outsiders will begin to think so. I've got city reporters calling me all day long, wanting to know the situation. People want to hear. And if they don't hear, they'll make something up. Maybe start to listen to how the State Chamber of Commerce feels about us. Their propaganda about Bolsheviki." He paused. "You do know I'm on your side—our people's side, the side of the community, Bill—anything

31

short of violence. I'd be hurt if you thought any different."

"We don't stand for violence in any form," Sneed said. "I'm hurt you'd think we do. And I'll be happy to tell you anything you want to know about the *closed* meeting, Hal, after it's over. Drop by the office tomorrow afternoon."

Bailey hung up the phone. Trovillion clicked his heels together, bowed and swept his hand toward Sneed. "Tom, the good senator needs your attention," he said.

Sneed hesitated. "I need to send a wire, Tom."

Bailey swept Trovillion's change off the counter and dropped it in the till then picked his way through the mess behind the counter to reach the telegraph. "That all you want, Hal?" he said.

"Not unless you have something more noble," Trovillion said.

"Not as far as you know."

"I know Danny Bayless was pulled out of a gutter behind the Ly-Mar Hotel last night, and he told me this very morning that the liquor that got him into that mess came from a certain news vendor who's late on his payments to the publisher of one of the finest small newspapers in the Midwest. Think of his family, Tom."

"Not in front of our elected officials," Tom said.

"'Course, I might stick around to see the contents of that telegram, if Curly will permit it."

"Nothing you'd be interested in," Sneed said. "Cora's condolences to some family back east. They lost their old father in a collapse in Pennsylvania."

"Funny, I didn't hear anything about that on the wire." Hal swallowed the last of a soda. "Odd, what with the work stoppage and all."

"It was a very small cave-in. A rabbit-hole operation. Look," Sneed said, digging in his suit pocket for the message. "Everything is on hold. Of course we're going to keep picketing Lester's mine, that much should be obvious, especially now they've cut the highway with their shovel and rerouted local traffic. Even the berry-pickers can't get back there anymore. I'm going to send this message and get some advice, is all, and if anything comes of it, I promise I'll bring it straight to you. First. Big exclusive."

Trovillion patted Sneed's shoulder pityingly and left.

Sneed swore young Bailey to secrecy, which he did every time he sent telegrams, knowing that every time Bailey leaked the contents. He gave him the message, to be sent to three parties, and waited as Bailey tapped it out.

> To: President Lewis, UMW of A; President Farrington, Illinois chapter UMW; President Gompers, AF of L.

> Is there an agreement by the American Federation of Labor that the Steam Shovel Men's Union have a right to man shovels to strip and load coal. Some here claim that they have jurisdiction, granted by mining department of American Federation of Labor. JW Tracy of Chicago, district representative of the International Steam Shovel Men's Union is furnishing men to load coal in the district. We do not believe the agreement exists. Wire answer after investigation. If agreement exists have authorities stop their men scabbing our coal miners at once. WJ Sneed, Sub-District President.

Sneed turned north on Park Avenue, walking past shops with their front plate windows shining flatly in the late sun. He stopped in the first deli north of the tracks to buy two pounds of mortadella and a dozen good hard rolls. Abramo wrapped the meat in waxed paper and then kraft paper and tied it all up neatly with twine. The rolls he placed carefully one-by-one into a paper bag using tongs. The old man spoke a Northern Italian dialect from some valley near Switzerland, Sneed had been told. Only the old-timers and some of the kids fresh off the boat could understand him. Sneed took the package and made a half-bow, feeling silly as he did so, and left. The old man called after him.

"Will be good," Abramo said. His eyes disappeared into the cracked leather of his face.

Sneed wasn't sure if he meant the mortadella or the strike. "Good," he said. "Buono, buono." Smiling, they parted. If nothing else, Sneed thought, the Lester situation has united us, Italian, Pole, Lithuanian, German, Scots, English. Even colored and white. A house divided not once but endlessly.

The Hughes, as Sneed thought of them, sat in the union office with their feet on a desk and their hats pitched back on their heads. Both smoked penny cigars and looked like Chicago gunmen. Sneed knew the truth: Fox Hughes, Sneed's sub-district vice-president, whined and groveled under his bosses and then bullied the men in the ranks. Brilliantined hair, checkered vest, imitation gold fob with a cut-glass charm hanging from it—a snake-oil and patent medicine man all the way to his marrow. Fox's father had been stabbed to death in a horse trade gone bad, and his sister worked the Ly-Mar, until Sneed made Fox relocate her up to East St. Louis. Sneed had had to explain why this was necessary. The man was good for running errands and working a barroom, and Sneed knew he could manage him, but he wondered what meanness Fox could sink to if he got a different master. Sneed tossed the meat and bread on the table, and the men tore at the packages eagerly.

Hugh Willis, the second of the Hughes, was a state board member of the union. Stuffed into his suit, a derby hat a size too small on his big head, Willis was a busybody and failed organizer who poked into every aspect of the locals' business under the pretense of looking out for the state board's interests. He was an actor, and dangerous because he had not settled into a role.

Sneed greeted the Hughes. Fox rose to his feet; Willis did not. Sneed asked what the latest word was and saw too late that Oldham Paisley, editor of the *Marion Republican*, sat in a dark corner under an electric stand fan.

Willis finally stood and posed majestically, aware of the audience provided by Paisley, Fox Hughes, Sneed, and three miners who had come in from a supply mission to feed union families. He declaimed, "Goddamn them, they ought to have known better than to come down here; but now that they're here, let them take what's coming to them."

Sneed turned red, and Fox carefully patted and petted Willis' arm to quiet him. The motions were wasted. Willis had nothing more in him; he had been sitting at the desk all afternoon inventing his lines, forgetting words, revising and repeating them until they were drilled into his head, waiting for the right moment to intone them. (Years later, after Americans had nearly forgotten Bloody Williamson County, Hugh Willis stood in dives on the Embarcadero with a shot in his hand and a beer on the counter, repeating that line to other drunks. When they didn't respond, he explained angrily why it was one of the illuminating moments of his life, and symbolic of an era in which working men had begun to forge a new, more equitable, and modern society.)

Sneed tried to say a few words to Paisley before he left the office. Perhaps he could keep Willis' jackassery off page one, anyway. But Sneed saw by the look on Paisley's face that he'd lost, and he smiled genuinely; he liked Paisley, Trovillion, and the others. They were smart, honest, good for conversing. The press might confuse things sometimes when what was needed most was a boost for the cause, but in the end, journalism would chronicle their triumph and create a record that others could look back on with pride and for instruction. Sneed shook Paisley's hand, shook his head at the Hughes, who were back at work on the meat and bread, and started walking home.

Oldham Paisley wrote down what Willis said and took it to the hot-type setter in the *Republican*'s offices in Marion. The three miners who happened to be in the office that day were from different parts of the county, and they took the little speech with them, if not in actual words, then in spirit, and as a contagion or a fire spreads, so did the spirit. Gossip and conjecture flooded over the borders of Jackson, Union, Saline, Hardin and Franklin Counties on the party-line telephone network. All across Little Egypt men and women, even those not associated with mining, ached to hear more. They left their homes and gathered in the streets in groups. The talk was delicious and anticipated something finally, actually, happening with regard to their work and pay. It didn't matter what might come of it. Even the talk raised fine hairs as when a good tenor sang beautifully.

Sneed paralleled the trolley tracks, passed the Rexall, the florist, Zwick's shoes, Bank of Herrin (big supporters), Esso station, Dale's Fixit Shop ("Why smash your thumbs when mine are so handy?"), and crossed over into the neighborhoods. Mostly Protestants lived south of the tracks, except for young Joe Van Buren, who owned the funeral parlor across the street from Sneed's own house and lived in an apartment above the visitation rooms. The steel tables, gallons of embalming fluid, hoses, knives, wigs and other accessories were kept in the basement, and corpses were slid down a wooden chute from the alley to his workshop. Joe had been in graves registration during the war.

Living in a charnel house, Sneed thought. War was one thing; many had done things they would never have to do again. Living one's life in the constant presence of death was another. He pitied the man: no wife, no children, not even a girl that he knew of, though Joe made good money. But what good was it? He seemed lonely and had often buttonholed Sneed to discuss, as neighbors, the fine points of organ removal or how to most easily double-dig the garden, when Sneed had no time or intent to dig anything ever again.

Van Buren had his faith, at least. Sneed thought it must be comforting to have a pathetical something to blame, curse, and beg for favor. He himself was a freethinker, though of course he attended Baptist services regularly. What could one do with the will to believe? It had been easier to democratize God than man.

Van Buren's bedroom window was on a level to Sneed's own, and Sneed could see him at night when Van Buren left the curtain open and the light on. Sneed wondered if Cora had ever noticed Van Buren standing there washing his face in the basin on his dresser.

Sneed thumbed the latch on his own front door. Studs and finials protruded from it; iron bands crossed it like bandoliers; long panes of leaded glass trisected the upper portion. The door looked like the bottom side of a castle drawbridge, and Sneed leaned heavily, wearily, on it to get inside.

"Cora," he called.

She emerged on the landing to the second floor in the dim light, dressed in gray wool high to the neck, the ivory brooch from her mother on her breast, hair in a tight bun at the base of her skull. She stepped to a vantage point over the foyer to watch him come in. Sneed was puzzled; she was the wife of a drowned sea captain, perhaps, but not the girl he'd married.

Funny, he thought, how some change completely without changing, and others stay the same behind their new gray hair and triple chins. Lisette, Romero the baker's wife, was still flirtatious and funny after forty years of rising early and wrestling dough, her shoulders and huge bosom rocking with the effort. Forty years of bentback painstaking production of bread. Sweeping up in the heat from the ovens, often ripely pregnant, year after year, eternally shiny with sweat. Romero had brought her to America on a sidewheel steamer in high seas, a rough passage that proved to be only a miniscule sample of the hardship to come. Yet still impudent, gleeful, filled to bursting with sweet treats and butter creams. Her children

36

made up a rhyme when they were young:

Cookies, cakes, cream pies,
No one's better fed than Mother and I.

Lisette roared at that, waving her baking peel like an artifact of war, saying, "You bet your bottom...and your dollar!"

When Romero married her she had been a great beauty, they said. All the men in Lombardy had wooed her, they said—Sneed found her curiously alluring still—but Romero, though poor at the time, had won her with a single bite of homemade cannelloni. It was remembered every year at their great anniversary parties where, surrounded by a dozen children, uncountable grandchildren, sisters, brothers, cousins, friends, customers, and all of us, Romero told the story, and Lisette always made the same joke as she raised her chianti to toast her children: "It wasn't his cannelloni that got us here, it was his penne!"

Cora didn't care for the Italians. Too boisterous, she said. Silly and loud. He still wanted to want Cora. They never discussed the girdles and trusses, but that wasn't it anyway. It was her mind or heart that had changed with their time together. She followed him, even insisted on it, but often bent to his will only after protracted argument. Worse, she did it so stridently, humorlessly, as if it were her only job to oppose him. His anger piled on itself, and then he said things. Both realized it was nothing. He felt guilty as sin for being cross, and he knew she was often right and acted for the benefit of the family. But he didn't like exercising the trait of visible anger. For a politician, it was career suicide. And a man wanted peace in his own home.

Cora stepped down the staircase in button-up shoes and lightly kissed him on the cheek.

"Dinner is warming, Will."

"Fine. I'm famished. Where are the children?"

"Carl is still out with his friends. Marjorie is drawing pictures of bugs in chalk on the back stoop."

"And the baby?"

"Asleep upstairs."

He looked up. "She's fine then?"

"Will, relax. She's two. She deserves a nap for all she did today."

"Won't that keep her up all night to sleep this late?"

"She'll sleep. And if she won't, I will sit up with her as I often do and read her stories. Right now we are very much involved with the Brothers Grimm."

"I'll check in on her after I eat."

"I'm sure she'd like that. And maybe Marjorie could have dessert with you?"

Will looked around strangely. The house felt different to him; there was a presence here tonight, hidden in the heavy draperies, the floor lamps, the dark walnut and chintz. He peered into the corners of the sitting room.

"Marjorie?" he said. "Where is Marjorie?"

"Out back, Will. I told you. What's the matter with you? Go and sit at the kitchen counter and I'll serve you both. You look tired."

"Not so tired. Still work to do."

"Tonight? You're working too much. It's not good for you. How can you be expected to please everyone?"

Will sipped coffee and read the paper as his sausage roll and beans heated. The columns of type calmed him since possibilities had concretized into facts. All the horses had run, no more money could be lost. The war to end all wars had been fought. But there were also hints of new catastrophes, still far away and mysterious.

Cora said, "I baked three sweet potato pies this morning. They're all gone but the slice I saved you. And a little for Marjorie. You want me to call her now?"

"Gone?" Will pulled his glasses off his face by a temple piece and rubbed his eyes and the sore spot where the glasses pinched. He felt the grit from his visit to the mine on his oily skin.

"Hungry vagrants. I told them to stay put and I'd get them something. They stayed put."

Will chuckled. "I'll bet they did."

"You know I'd never let a thief size up this house. They were just hungry men, and I gave a half-dozen of them slices of pie, and they stood and ate their food on the steps. Some asked for glasses of cold water, and I got that too. The first ones I was able to send off with bread and a piece of potato too, but I had to save something for ourselves."

"Were there any union men begging, Cora?"

"A few admitted they were. They said they'd take the food to their families. That drinker was here. The one you say has opportunities but won't work."

"Jansen. He's learned to live on crusts. You could have given everything to the others, I wouldn't care. Start with the silver."

"Don't be ridiculous."

"Okay, but it's more important this time, Cora, and there'll be hell to pay if it all goes sour. Did I tell you the New York papers wrote us up as the single greatest bastion of union miners in the country? Thirty thousand of us in just two counties, let alone the others, and one hundred percent membership. People are watching us closely. We're the heart of this whole country's workers, all under the same pressures."

Cora said, "You have to be here for *us*, Will. Tell them that too?"

"What else could I tell them?" he said, missing her meaning.

"The labor struggle is important, don't get me wrong," she said. "If what happened at Pana or in Colorado happened here, I think sometimes our whole world could change. I read one time how the Mississippi ran backwards for three days after the New Madrid quake. This could become that kind of movement, something terrifying and disastrous. Another Civil War, Will. Anarchy. The very thought of it scares me. It's fine you're doing your job, but you have to be here for your family, too."

Cora saw the distaste on his face and, afraid it would lead to her denunciation, added, "If we break and scatter, what hope is there for the rest of them?"

Will smiled. "My own Mother Jones. 'To ensure we have no brainsick brain workers nor heart-sick hand workers.' Eh, Mother? I'm proud of you, Tooks."

Will kissed her forehead, rose and went to the back of the house to his study, where he shut the pocket doors and locked them, forgetting about sweet-potato pie and his daughter Marjorie, even as Cora was behind the house pulling the girl up from her chalk drawings. Cora threatened her with the cure—three drops of coal oil on a teaspoon of sugar—if she didn't shake a leg. She thought she'd make tea for them too, since Will never had much chance to spend time with his children.

The floorboards creaked as Sneed went to the window in his study. The new enclosed hallway to the privy, sided and painted to match the house, partially blocked his view of Doc's house. Doc, his cousin by marriage, was prospering, even though he almost lost his practice when he was away with the Dental Corps in France. Sneed remembered the treadle he himself had pumped for a dentist...almost 25 years ago now. He wondered if he'd done everything he might have in that time. Had he read enough? Traveled as he could? Loved, or been loved? His tongue ran around the inside of his mouth and found the hole from the wisdom tooth. Coming to with Doc's knee in his chest in the stink of chloroform, Doc straining and red in the face, blood everywhere, trying to pull the shattered tooth that had grown an extra root and refused to come out of the jaw. Doc said, "Oh you're back with us," and continued to work.

His entire life spent trying to put things right after the disaster of parental death. To feel like it was worth it, to feel satisfied. It—life—had taken such a toll, such large amounts of energy, a monstrous will, and so often those who loved you, who would most benefit from your actions, fighting you every last step of the way.

He knew he must get this speech right. Everyone looked to him for leadership, and their enemies watched for weakness, and the country held its breath in anticipation. He thought he might start with a history lesson. The rights of Man. Whatever it was, he shouldn't mention an author but make it sound like a man had said it to him in a bowling alley three days ago.

That old German with his alienated labor, the impossible return to organic connection to the fruits of labor. Not far off Thoreau, funnily enough. You could try to live a certain way, like Three-Piece, who made fine editions of the love letters of dead kings with his artsy Morris-style book press, but it wasn't a living.

Where it mattered, the shift of power had been to men who knew nothing of craft. *Managers, managing only to stuff their pockets with money that*...no. Some of those men would be there tomorrow. Jefferson had some bit about those laboring in the earth being the chosen people of God. Hypocritical old deist probably went whoring with Paine after he wrote it.

Inclusion was key, and it was almost too easy in that sense. Usually there were strained relations between the Italians, Americans, Bulgarians, Hungarians, Scots, Irish, Welsh, even a few Syrian tradesmen. MacCormack's stupid demands to put a law on the books to keep Negroes out of Herrin after sundown. But this time, they had a simple and common target: an out-of-towner with money, defying us and the agreement we made with him.

"It will be not only possible but also necessary for Labor and Capital to be equals at the table. It takes generations to implant dignity in the human breast, but once planted, it's ineradicable. Small gains over time, we're off our knees and walking; we will no longer crawl."

And Lester cut us out by bringing in scab labor when we magnanimously—no, say "kindly"—*gave him permission to dig and load that coal, with the proviso*—say: *"as long as"*—*he didn't ship it. He'd make plenty by having it ready to ship quickly, once a nationwide agreement was reached.*

Were we wrong in that? Many of the men fought me on it, that's for sure.

Sneed paced the study. His mind raced, he felt confused, even dizzy. What should he propose? What was he advocating? Sally and Bullyrag in embrace came to mind, Doc and Lena House, Van Buren in his lonely room, the new English teacher at Southside Elementary, a Miss Scherer. Helen, his baby daughter, asleep on a child-size bed with a light blanket on her pudgy legs.

We must build forums first, in order to build systems, in which Right Action can take place. Ours is the search for Emerson's point d'appui—say "bedrock"—a foundation unconditional and absolute, where we can build a society to last.

He sat in the rolling armchair at his desk and picked aimlessly at the contents of the dozen pigeonholes, opened drawers mindlessly, shut them, moved papers about. Opened a different drawer, found real Amontillado sherry disguised in a cologne bottle and replaced it. Found his Smith & Wesson revolver forgotten years earlier. He opened the cylinder. Six bullets still in place. Who had he thought they were for? Someone who would take what he had, back when the community was safer than now, and he had no enemies, and he owned next to nothing? After the war, when things got a little rougher, he never even thought to have a weapon at hand, and the thing had gotten pushed deeper into the drawer each year. Funny. He'd gone right to it. He left it on top of his desk and reached for a book instead.

Platitudes, parables, abstractions. *If a man owns land, the land owns him.* That one wasn't bad. But would it mean Lester belongs to us because we *are* the land? Or that we have been kept from becoming whole and

41

self-reliant? Most of them would hear only the cadences anyway, so the trick was to skein threads of easy understanding into the rhetoric. *We must not* start *this*.

He paced, allowed Cora to bring him tea, wrote notes, muttered, tore the notes in pieces and began again. He thought of John Mitchell, his mentor, dead now three years. Maybe he could use some of that:

"Workingmen have learned to strike without violence, hold together through thick and thin, to pay dues, to make sacrifices, to obey orders, to stand shoulder to shoulder and to abide the issue of industrial conflict. This is how the public is educated to an appreciation of labor. Only 50 years ago, unions were denounced as immoral, and only slowly has that changed into honor."

At eleven Cora tap-tapped on the door and asked if he was coming to bed.

"I can't just yet."

"You have to think of your health, Will."

"I have to think of how I'm going to speak to a group of scared and angry men tomorrow morning."

"Why don't you come off to bed now and get up early? You can finish then."

"Because the job is not done yet. Why can't you ever understand that? You married me knowing all this, and you do seem to enjoy what comes of it, so why are you asking me to stop when there is no alternative, since you only distract me and make me feel worse and delay me even longer?"

"Actually, I didn't know it would be like this when I married you," Cora said. "Not that it's bad. But I had no idea then. Good night."

"Good night, Cora. Wait. I'm sorry. Love you. I'll be up soon as I can."

"The union will prosper as long as it respects the will of the people, that great, humane public justice."

Was that true? Or did failed movements fail because they didn't contain the means for self-propagation? Jefferson again: No hidden genius. Maybe the self-taught could *never* be in touch with the main thing.

Two hours later, he believed he was ready. He couldn't tell anymore. So many side issues to avoid, insoluble in themselves. Jobs lost to the machines, young people lost to cities. Tales of wealth about the very people supposed to be looking out for the workers. He looked around his study at the walls of bookshelves crammed to overflowing. A graveyard of dead ideas, clothing cast off by unfamiliar guests. Utterly useless yet nothing else to this life.

Painful, he thought. Not that he had been young and ignorant, but rather that he wasn't young anymore when he caught fire with the consciousness that should have sparked a dozen years earlier. Where had he been all those years? Just living. Worse, just alive. Reverend Meeker of the Presbyterian Church was a former classmate of Woodrow Wilson's and a Princeton Seminary graduate, but Sneed labored through correspondence packets from the Miners' and Mechanics' Institute. Those early letters he'd written were still an embarrassment: "I was shure some glad...." He'd destroyed his own and wondered if it would be going too far to send a man to get them from their recipients' files. John Walker had shown Sneed a letter he'd written Mother Jones on Sneed's behalf, and her encouraging reply, so Walker had no problem sharing private mail.

He slipped his shoes off and walked along the baseboards to the kitchen to ring Wallace, who pulled up ten minutes later.

"Where to, Mr. Sneed?"

Sneed, in the back seat, looked at the young man's profile. Ruby could have done worse, especially with her temperament. Wild as some wop. Looked like one too. It might have led to embarrassment. Wallace was polite, prompt and loyal. Good-looking. And he was a hard bastard, deep down. His daddy, Judge Duncan, was a hard bastard too. Good men.

"Thought it would be nice to have a cocktail before I turn in, Wallace. Big day tomorrow, so don't let me stay out too late."

"Yessir."

"I'd buy you a drink too, Wallace, but I don't think you could drink a whole one."

Wallace just grinned and worked the gears. Sneed remembered after he said it that he'd said it in this exact setting many times before, but the kid was fine, and Sneed felt like a tired, accomplished leader of men. He sat back and relaxed, allowing his eidetic memory to bring back women in Herrin, Springfield, Chicago, Washington. Each town a transmigration of political beings across geography.

And while his state senate district was a little rough, he could still accomplish anything—U.S. Congress, Department of Labor, diplomatic corps. He'd often thought that Cora could have been anyone's wife. She was smart and capable and didn't suffer from being too good all the time. Maybe he could be an ambassador.

He'd seen picture books on Versailles and read of perfumed sheep in the courtyard of Marie's faux hameau there. Now there was a culture. Cheese smelled like armpits and the barnyard of eau-de-cologne. He could use that in the right crowd as a parable of false sensibilities. *The rich can't stop themselves from imitating the poor once they have them well-and-good subjugated. What's next, brown bread?*

They passed the lights of Herrin. The powerful engine, the headlights pointing the way, and the young Trooper at the wheel relaxed him.

During the war he'd taken a ten-day leave from Number 7 to organize for the first time, and he'd worried for his awful job. The ten days expired and another two weeks passed, but there was still nothing settled with that fluorspar mob down on the river. Even the boys had been able to work the steamboats, hew ties, pick berries on a farm, but he had nothing coming in. Cora had been on him for that, and the Sheriff and his gunmen were waiting for him the last time he got off the boat in Elizabethtown. He'd thought it all bigger than anything anybody had ever done. That, at least, came with age: knowing the actual size of the venture you were involved in.

He'd been a kid in a grown man's body, an innocent no better than some beast, but even then his voice had power. As he was giving that one speech the boys started slipping out one-by-one and he just kept giving them the stuff about the fight until there was nobody to say it to. When he and Edna were leaving town they heard the first rocks rolling off the rooftops of the bunch against them and by god what a thrilling sound that was.

Farrington had offered him UMW International Organizer after that. Sumbitch was about half-illiterate himself, but you always looked up, it was just a matter of to whom. He knew now that Farrington's were form letters, but how right they were for him at that point in his development.

"Bill, I am glad to know that you have got an opportunity to enter the labor service, and believe that you should accept, because while it is discouraging, and at times, very trying, and all the time it requires hard

work and a good deal of sacrifice, still there is nothing in the world a man can do that will make do much for the common good and bring so much satisfaction to him himself, than doing that work; and I know that no matter what position you may be in you will be clean and straight to the end, doing the best you can. I know that no matter what you do, Brother Snead, you will do it because you think it is the right thing to do."

Crossing over in Colp: Shelley's tiny cottage among the Negro dwellings. She had never worked the houses, he'd checked into it, but oh Jesus toomanywomen.

Cora lay in bed as the noise of the car diminished on the empty wet street. She sat up, startled and confused, as if wakened suddenly, though she had not been asleep. She felt like getting out of her bed and running somewhere, fleeing. But this was *her* solid house with three courses of laid brick and children lying under its roof. She lay back, couldn't breathe, got up and opened the window. It was only the asthma, though she felt as if she might drown sometimes in the thick scent of lilac planted too close to the foundation. She stood, terrified, trying to breathe, and looked at the darkened funeral home across the street, an outdated Victorian with turrets and bay windows like on Daddy and Momma's house.

It wasn't that she'd thought they'd live forever. She knew all along she'd be left alone one day. But so many years passed after she'd first worried about death that she began to think it was childish to dread it, or anything at all. Then suddenly they were gone, and a whole generation with them, and the rest of the extended family scattered. *Then* she'd known a deeper and more terrible loneliness than any child, despite her extravagant fears, could ever have imagined, thank God.

Chapter Four

At dawn O'Rourke saw what he was in for. In a strip mine nothing was buried, so there could be no secrets. The camp sat in the middle of flat scrublands, twenty-five acres of sandy dirt that covered layers of clay, loose rocks and shale. The overburden had been stripped away by a Bucyrus steam shovel like the one TR posed in when they were digging the Canal, and a satin seam of raw coal ran along the bottom of the twenty-foot deep trench for half a mile. Various workshops, shacks, and outbuildings stood along one side of the trench; on the other a spur of track came in from the main line for rolling stock. A smaller shovel leaned in and hacked at the coal and swung it into cars without sorting it. A third shovel sat with its engine dismantled on a tarp and its bucket slack-jawed in the dirt like an exhausted beast. It was even grimmer than he'd imagined. The hangover didn't help.

O'Rourke asked at the cookhouse for McDowell, the mine super-intendent, who walked out of his office with a furious limp. O'Rourke had already decided he was too ill to be moved back to Chicago and had planned to stick around for a day or two, and when he saw McDowell's wooden leg and glower, he introduced himself meekly, said he was glad to be there, and where could he be of use? McDowell looked at him suspiciously but introduced him perfunctorily to his assistant and a series of steam shovel engineers, oilers and various workmen in the camp. A rusting Burlington Northern engine faced the bumper at the end of the spur, still coupled to the seven cars in its train. Two of these were bunkhouses, another was O'Rourke's office, quarters and warehouse for dry goods, food, extra tools and parts, and the others were for coal.

O'Rourke sneered at the men's accommodations in preparation for complaining about his own. The way their bunks were stacked one on another like racks on a ship, they couldn't even sit up, and they had no electric lights. McDowell cut him short. If the men were not sleeping, they should be working, he said. This was a mining camp, not the Great Northern Hotel. As he sorted out the keys for the doors and file cabinets that would be O'Rourke's responsibility, McDowell admitted that most in camp were just maintaining equipment and standing by to go back to work. Unless an agreement between coal operators and the union was reached, or they got special permission to ship the coal on hand, there was little to do. He turned over the keys to O'Rourke, who immediately felt more cheerful with this inheritance, and as soon as McDowell had limped off, O'Rourke began to rifle through the contents of the commissary.

The rest of the morning O'Rourke kept to himself in the safety of his own boxcar, except for four visits to the mess kitchen. He had nothing more than water and coffee there, even though Malkovaich, who was the cook, begged him to eat something so he'd be rid of food that was going bad. By noon O'Rourke was feeling much, much better and began helping Malkovaich out. O'Rourke lazed in his office in the boxcar. He had come to do just this.

By mid-afternoon he felt restless. He thought of the girl, Mercy, three hundred miles away. She'd be dancing and meeting new people tonight. He thought about taking a nap but wasn't tired because he hadn't done anything. He got up and scratched out a Hello, remember me, bet you never thought I'd actually write did you? note to her.

Despite the employment agency's cut, he made good money. What woman wouldn't want to hear that? His arrangement also included room and board—neither anything to write home about, though he told her— so he was free to do with his money what he chose. He didn't trust any hayseed bank so he'd keep his paychecks in his wallet, and his wallet in the back pocket of his pants, and his pants on at all times, even when he slept, though he didn't tell Mercy that. The checks would go straight in with his other investments. He didn't tell Mercy about those either, not yet, until he knew she could be trusted.

Old Man Haskel had called him trustworthy. And clever. Haskel always said, Irishmen are very clever. It was a fetish with that guy. But O'Rourke found files in Haskel's office because he organized everything to his own clever system, and his witty comments about the office were tired sarcasm and barroom punchlines. At these, Haskel had laughed, and the more disdainful and cynical O'Rourke became, the more Haskel loved him. O'Rourke was baffled he could give no offense. If anyone was to blame it was the old man for being a goddamned fool and for piling so much responsibility on such a young man. O'Rourke would turn thirty-two soon. Thirty-three.

He bet the old man wasn't laughing now. It was a disappointment not to see for himself, but he might still read of what he'd done in the *Trib*. It had been enough to get out whole.

He had resigned from Haskel's on a cold sunny day in Chicago with a thirty mile-per-hour straight wind off the lake. A mongrel trotted up the sidewalk in front of him, propelled along Wabash by the bow wave of O'Rourke's hurry and the smell of tripe and butter beans from Finn's. He felt a strange pity for the bitch with its worn-out teats and patches of mange, but its own mood was so gay that he pulled himself from depression and nodded manfully to the brain-addled boxer named Mouse at the door and went through to the back.

"Well?" Leo asked.

"Greatest country in the world, America," O'Rourke said, tossing his coat down into the seat as if it and nothing else was of great consequence to him; the world was all easy days.

"How's that?" Leo said. He leaned back in the dark pine booth, his nearly bald head spotted with age and sun spots, smiling coyly and twining his fingers over his belly. "I thought you paid me to tell *you* what's great."

"I was just going to say that in America you get to choose your associates. And I choose to become acquainted with the upper class."

Leo snorted and waved two fingers at the waiter. "Surely you can aim for better than that, O'Rourke. Listen to me. Take a minute one day and watch these golem marching up Michigan Avenue and being driven in from Hyde Park with their heads held like this. And their dead eyes. I'm serious: one of them stopped me on the street the other day. You should have heard him. 'I'm going to tell you a story,' he said. And then he gave me ten minutes of what he ate for breakfast!"

Leo gleefully hit the table so hard that O'Rourke jumped.

The waiter expertly avoided Leo's plump fist and poured the drinks.

"Liver, rare," O'Rourke said.

Leo looked smug, as if amused that O'Rourke should need to eat, and shook his head at the waiter in some way that suggested the waiter knew all about it.

"I'll tell you, O'Rourke. These guys think I work for them. But I watch their markets for me. I can tell you within 10 cents what I'm worth right now. I told this guy that the other day, and he couldn't believe it. 'How could you know that?' he asked me. How could I *not* know, I said to him. There's a new millionaire every day."

O'Rourke nodded, unable to follow. He wasn't sure Leo's wisdom wasn't just age, booze or stupidity, but he figured he had best make sure. On a personal level he couldn't help liking Leo, especially for his certainty. Certainty breeds competence, Leo had said many times. Or maybe he said confidence. In any case, O'Rourke knew a good fence was hard to find.

"Can't you picture living off interest, Leo? Maybe investing the interest too. If it was me, I'd spend the day reading the paper in Grant Park and feeding birds. Walk up to the Water Tower and turn around and walk all the way back to Soldier Field." He could see Leo's interest flagging.

"What would you do, Leo?"

Leo crossed his leg and leaned back from his gin. He wore no socks under his wingtips, and his ankles were swollen tight.

"Those park benches and long walks are what you do six months of the year anyway, O'Rourke."

O'Rourke grinned, unsure.

"Maybe even more if you meet the right woman," Leo said.

Was he being complimentary or perverse? In his discomfort and excitement, O'Rourke said, "Oh, you know the bootblack on the corner by the Berghoff?"

The old man looked amused and propped his elbow on the back of the bench, as if he knew everything O'Rourke knew. O'Rourke felt nervous and happy.

"He said to look at U.S. Steamship," O'Rourke said. "Timmy whispered it to a guy I seen down there before. What do you think?" He hesitated over the word "seen," wondering if it had been too much.

Leo sighed and rubbed his eye with the back of his fist like a sleepy boy, but when he slicked back strands of oily gray hair in the next practiced

49

motion, his hard, cunning face was a revelation.

"I've got two hot ones and we'll go with those," he said, slipping the envelope O'Rourke handed him into his coat pocket. "The problem with the world as it is is that bootblacks won't humble themselves to be bootblacks without trying to be something else too. Everybody in America wants something else."

O'Rourke sat waiting for his liver and onions, feeling like a failure for having his thoughts wrong. He wished he had something else to offer the older man but nothing much came to mind.

"I guess I should just get out of town for a while," he said finally, imagining Leo would think that was the smart play. "Maybe I should get some of that back from you and really head out. Denver. New Orleans. I don't know."

The thought of those towns filled him with lonely dread. He didn't know much about Leo—he'd mentioned a wife and two successful sons, though O'Rourke couldn't recall what their successes had entailed—but he felt, deep in his gut, that it would be right and proper to be a part of his family.

"You are a lucky young man," Leo said. His smile did not curve upward but framed a square of four crooked teeth, and he looked like a very large prairie dog sitting upright in the booth. "It's already taken care of. My buddy said come and see him."

O'Rourke brightened. "You mentioned me to someone?"

"Goddamned right I mentioned. Did I not say I'd take care of you? Go to this address, tell Frank I'm the one sent you. And you won't be needing any of this, either," Leo said, patting his pocket. "Go now, before they hire somebody. I'll take care of that lunch you ordered."

O'Rourke walked briskly and directly to the employment agency. He could think of only two demands: few duties and decent pay. He was willing to give on the pay if room and board were thrown in, but he really didn't intend to work. Of course it had to be out of town, what with Haskel and all. Night watchman at one of those medicinal breweries in Milwaukee would be just the sort of thing. Leo was a good man, for a crook, and it had been nice of him. O'Rourke thought of him in vaguely fatherly terms, though he had never had a father and didn't know what the experience was meant to be like. O'Rourke wondered if a man was always afraid of his father.

"Leo who?" the woman at the employment agency asked. "Frank who?" She wore a felt hat with a balding feather and a raincoat, as if she intended to leave the office immediately. She dabbed at her drooping lids where too much white showed below her pupils.

O'Rourke slumped on the counter and explained himself.

"My Phil didn't know any Leos or Franks, I'm sure of that, Hon. Now if you're looking for work, I can help. Otherwise, I got things to do...."

O'Rourke thought for only a second; he had no ready cash, no hope of work, and Haskel would have the ward boss's goons out looking for him soon. Maybe they'd already begun. He cautiously allowed the old woman to tell him what was available. The job not only met his demands, the pay was so good O'Rourke became immediately suspicious.

"This is accounting, right? I'm not looking to labor."

"There's nothing about accounting," she said. "It says here 'Clerk.'"

O'Rourke grimaced at his watch. At the very least Haskel's auditors would be sorting through the mess he'd made to cover his tracks. He suddenly remembered he'd forgotten to remove his home address from his own file.

"How long will my services...?"

"There's no contract, Hon. All our work is open-ended due to the lack of an agreement. Could be two days, could be two years. You never know with those people."

"A strike?" O'Rourke said, angry again that the situation was too complicated to grasp at once. "What people?"

"Miners, doll." She stopped writing and looked at him over her glasses. "Coal miners. Mr. Lester needs to keep things running." She looked O'Rourke over more carefully and smiled charmingly with her gray teeth. "But don't be scared."

"Who's scared?" O'Rourke said testily. "Do I look scared?" He wasn't even clear on what he should be scared of, but no old bitch was going to call him chicken....

"Relax. You don't look like the Pinkerton type, that's all. Calm down."

O'Rourke, mollified, nodded in silent agreement. He had taken guff from a string of half-wit bosses like any other worker. He'd been at Haymarket; it's where he ate his lunch most days when he ran numbers in the area several years earlier. Not that he had pretensions, either, which is why he'd never gone to college.

Yes, he saw instantly, being an armed strikebreaker would be wrong, though he would make a good one, and for a brief moment he felt in his limbs the joy of striking someone who really deserved it. With an ax handle, maybe. His muscles twitched at the thought, like they might in a dream of falling. But he wasn't like that, he reminded himself, and taking on those responsibilities would open the way to dangers he simply didn't want or need right now—they were complications in an otherwise perfect plan.

Crunching numbers wouldn't align him with Pinkertons and headbusters. Even a herd of local brutes would be smart enough to see the difference in that. He could hear himself lecturing those people—those coal miners in that dark southern region:

Conflict and struggle, brothers, are necessary to improve life, but some, such as myself, choose to go around the entire class issue with guile and nerve. Most people do not have the creativity or mental capacity to do this, and so you make your choices and take your stands. Bully for you. But I cannot martyr myself for your cause, this is not my fight, you see, and that is why, gentlemen, you must stand aside now and let me pass.... Thank you.

He took the job, just for the immediate future, the one part of his life he was really invested in.

Swinging along Wells, happy in his overall good fortune—it had been a good day, despite his vague uneasiness at Leo's confusion over names—O'Rourke caught the sly and overly-conscious glance of a shop girl through the large window that fronted her store. He stopped walking as if he had been switched off. There was nothing dramatic or thoughtful in it; he just stopped. He was aware of the chance he took by not returning immediately to his room to gather his things but did not wonder at stopping.

The customer in front of the counter couldn't decide between the bolt of yellow print or the bolt of pink print fabric for her daughter's recital, it was Friday and there would be no time to start over if the first choice was a misstep and then she would be out the money too and even if her friend's sister was the seamstress she would have to be paid she just didn't know. O'Rourke stood behind the older woman, grinning and mimicking her. The counter girl bit her lips, and he knew he'd made the right play. The girl measured out the cloth by pulling it repeatedly to arms' length, flexing her chest, and taking up her scissors, she cut the bolt off square with strong fingers. O'Rourke fidgeted with impatience as she folded and wrapped the cloth, dragging out the transaction with little courtesies and nonsense questions. After years of digging for coins in her pocketbook, the old broad took her purchase and left.

"Can I help, sir?" the girl said innocently.

She understood full well he wanted no linen, no gingham; that the lace, ribbons, bows, ties, snaps, buttons and walls of thread spools meant nothing to him. In fact, the chemical stench from the fabrics was making his eyes and the inside of his nose burn, so he worked more quickly than he knew he should, especially given the game she'd been playing at stalling with the customer. Immediately he was rebuffed, but even in her angry reaction he knew he had her figured correctly. Business was slow, and he was persistent, trying to make the play slightly boring so she'd grow tired of it but not of him, a delicate task that required an artist's touch.

"I'll agree to a drink," she finally said, and he congratulated himself for persevering. "But only after you've come in the shop some other time. That is, if I'm free. I don't even know you," she said and pouted, long ringlets on either side of her head bobbing like springs.

O'Rourke guessed that the shop belonged to her father.

"Why, yes," she said. "Father owns two. We live above this one."

"Good," O'Rourke said. He felt the surety of genius in action.

"Why good?" the girl asked. She looked worried.

"Because I know where you work, and I know where you live, Mercy," O'Rourke said. "So remember what you said about next time. Because next time I come in this shop, I will say...."

With this, O'Rourke turned from the girl, walked out the door and down the block to the corner, where he knew she could still see him through the plate window. He did an about-face and marched back into the store.

"I will say that this *is* the next time, and I'm holding you to your promise," he said.

She laughed at that, tongue red from cherry candy. "You cheat," she said. "All bets are off."

He sobered suddenly and explained to her for the first time in earnest how he really was leaving the next morning, that he had appointments before that, but they sure might have had fun. The regret came up in her eyes, it was wonderful to know he'd won, and the shop seemed to disappear as he flashed forward to the heat of her face and taste of her spit.

She promised she'd write if he would. This commitment made the conversation awkward and slow until he invented a tale about where he was going. Later he couldn't remember what he had said but thought maybe it was Memphis. She responded with a story about a boy that O'Rourke knew was a lie because nobody in her crowd would have that much money. They compared experiences in the dance halls, and he really had to go.

In the final strained silence before he went, she turned and ran to the back of the shop and up a flight of dull-thudding stairs. He heard her overhead, sliding open and slamming shut drawers. She returned with a small photograph of herself in a cardboard folder. In the photo she looked stern and much older. He stepped behind the counter to get it, and Mercy collided with him. She kept her eyes open, watching the door and pushed him away just before the next customer came in.

O'Rourke swaggered out, sure he wouldn't be gone long enough to write. Anyway, writing was for suckers. He reached his building, checked for detectives in the alley and the stairwells, and safely packed a bag and a box that held all he owned. He spent the rest of the night at a card game to raise some traveling cash, where he bragged about the girl he'd made until one of the near-professional players threatened, You better shut up about that pig-meat or else. O'Rourke lost most of his remaining money and fell asleep in a corner.

The next morning, with his cardboard suitcase gone fuzzy at the corners and a box of office supplies from Haskel's, O'Rourke boarded a train at Union Station. He fell asleep from boredom and anxiety before the train ever left the station and napped as long as he could, wanting the trip over and done with. He forced himself to ignore the sound and movement of those around him and fell back to sleep each time. But by noon the trip had become a purgatory of layovers in every rural station on the track. The train had no toilet or drinking water, and the stations were either locked or were simple waiting rooms with a couple of crude benches.

How, he wondered, could farmers have nothing for him to eat? In the city there was always something doing. That tavern with the Polish sausage in those buns, split, brushed with butter and toasted on the grill? Christ, and kraut. And a cold beer pulled fresh from the keg in the cool basement. German potato salad with the bacon in it and a hunk of dinner roll. He could have eaten three of the bologna sandwiches they smashed and fried on the griddle around the corner from his place—his former place, he thought nostalgically, now he'd sneaked down the fire escape in the dark and stiffed them on two months rent. Dangerous, yes, but courageous. Coal miners had nothing on the super of *that* dump.

His only meal that day, as he thought of it self-pityingly, was some rotgut hidden in his suitcase. By the time he remembered it, the bottle had leaked on his clothes, and though he didn't want it he thought he'd finish it rather than let it go to waste. The whiskey burned his throat and empty stomach and rose up again as gorge that he swallowed back down, which made him belch, and that brought the fire up again. He hadn't wanted it, and it made him angry that it worked against him.

The towns got smaller and more isolated as the train crept downstate. He began to dread the string of jarring thumps of cars colliding in succession when the engine slowed. They pulled into Tuscola, then Arcola.

"You know what the wag asked," he said aloud to the conductor taking tickets. "What's next, Coca-Cola?"

The conductor ignored him while other passengers stared.

"Actually, mister," a young man with a new hat said seriously. "It ain't Coca-Cola. It woulda been Champaign going the other way. Going this way, there ain't no joke."

O'Rourke shuffled a deck of cards mindlessly, cut and re-cut them, fanned and shot them from right to left hand. He picked them off the floor. He ordered them again and held the deck up to his fellow passengers, but the rubes weren't having any. O'Rourke felt their stares. He sat up, so straight that his back muscles gave out and he slumped against the window moodily. The men stared. He knew so before he looked, and when he finally looked they were staring, dumb and impassive as beasts with no real threat in their eyes, just a flat gaze that filled him with incredulous rage at their judgment. He tried to outstare them but failed; their workworn faces and honest clothes reproached him for trying. O'Rourke glanced pointedly at someone's dirt-scaled boots, hoping the man would feel shame. His own shoes were uncomfortably hot, as if the floor of the compartment had heated up, and his shanks itched uncontrollably. One of the farmers coughed into a rose of bandanna, and further up the car a baby cried over the deeper murmur of its mother's voice. O'Rourke felt panicked, sick, and stared out at a giant pin oak standing as solid in a fleeting bean field as if it had always been there and always would be. Somehow the idea of that permanence drew whiskey-laced bile into his throat where it burned him again.

Now he leaned back in the caster chair in his very own office with the half-written letter to Mercy in front of him. The memory of that whiskey made him feel peaked again with the effects of the night before and the two full dinners he'd eaten since noon, and he slid onto his cot and stayed there into the evening, rising only when a miner needed something from stores. He got the item or paperwork at his own speed then returned to his cot.

O'Rourke knew he had a good deal and began to wonder when it would be safe to return to the city. Part of that would depend on Leo and the investments he made.

He tried to lull himself to sleep with fantasies of a harem, oiled girls squirming in piles in a tent on the desert, then of a former landlady, Mrs. Latimer, who had to care for him because, oh, he had a fever, but suddenly revealed herself and forced him to diddle her. There was something vaguely unsatisfying in these reveries, and he wondered if he was coming down with something. He rose to finish the letter to Mercy, felt as if something was at odds there too, and scribbled a quick ending without thought. He sealed it in an envelope without reading it again and tossed it in the basket for pickup.

Malkovaich asked if he was going on the nightly outing, and O'Rourke rousted himself to climb into the mine truck, but only after Malkovaich assured him they were not going to Ma Hatchett's. At Freddy Jerk's, on the other side of Herrin, far from Colp, O'Rourke sipped carefully at one ginger ale, listened to the band and chatted briefly with Malkovaich about Virginia Rappe's death. In O'Rourke's opinion, Fatty Arbuckle was guilty. You couldn't trust somebody who kept saying he was innocent. He knew about himself that he didn't always make the smart play, but he would do so now and his life would become familiar and predictable. That, he thought, must be the most comforting and sensible thing money could buy.

CHAPTER FIVE

Wallace pulled up outside and honked three times. Bill, dog-tired, groaned and said Do I have to? Shelley said, You don't have to go, but you can't stay here and gave him some incentive to come awake. Damn, he said. Oh. Jesus Shelley. She stopped of a sudden.

"What?" he asked, incredulous.

"Did you make my brother a deputy sheriff or did he get it on his own?"

"You were thinking of your brother just now?"

"How'd John Stallons get to be street commissioner?"

"Come on."

"Best tell me. Wallace is waiting, and so's your wife."

"How would I make him a deputy? I'm State. He works for the town."

"But you can make things happen."

"So can you."

She worked on him a while longer but when he tensed she stopped.

"Oh no."

"How would Jeremy become a lawyer?"

"You've got to be kidding me." He sat up.

"You look angry. So does that."

"Stop playing around. There's no place in Southern Illinois a colored man can do any such thing. You know that."

"Yeah, but what about Chicago, or Memphis, or out east? What about those places you were talking about last night?"

"Finish and I'll tell you."

"Tell and I'll finish."

He laughed and began to dress. She said no, no and tried to pull him out of his clothes as he put them on. At first it was a game, but it started to get a little rough.

"I'm sorry, baby," she said. "Come on back here tonight. I'll kill you with kindness, I promise."

"Seems to be the prevailing sentiment these days."

"I'm sorry."

He held her face in his palms and kissed the top of her head.

"You okay for the rest of the month?" he said.

"Sure, sure. Go on. Hey: here's your hat; what's your hurry?"

"See you soon, Shelley."

"Be good," she called as the door was shutting.

Shelley Brown brushed her hair, stopped and looked in the mirror. That kohl he liked was a killer. She rolled her eyes, squinted hard so tears came out. Must be having flapper fantasies, thinking of someone else, but no harm in that.

Didn't leave much of a trace. The bed was more mussed than normal, imprint of another head on the pillows. Lingering cologne, sex. She sponged off standing in a washtub. Cold water rolled down her armpits, breasts, sides, legs. She wiped between her legs and looked at the sponge. Strange how it went so fast from slick to sticky. Her period was coming— breasts tender, though she hadn't told him that—and she knew she was safe.

Man like that had a lot to protect. Mama had cleaned his house and it wore her out. She said that white lady—at the time Shelley had had no reason to pay attention to the name—never gave it a chance to get dirty, but there was a lot of house there and she oversaw every detail. She told Mama, who knew best, that dirt and grit wore out the floors and carpets and it was a duty to keep things clean so they lasted. Shelley had gone with her Mama one time to collect her pay, and Shelley remembered a cut glass chandelier over a long long dining room table. At the time all she could think was: poor Mama, she's got to clean every little piece of that diamond light with its thousands of facets.

Shelley pulled the sheet up, folded down the top and tucked the corners under. She tied back the curtains and threw open the windows. That was after Daddy died the way they all did, if they weren't crushed or gassed or blown up, hacking against the black sputum in his barreled

58

chest. Mama went to work for anybody could pay to make the trip from Colp worthwhile. Back and forth, seven days a week. And if the mines weren't running and a truck wasn't going into town, Mama used to hoof it, eight miles, and have to apologize if she got there late.

When Bill was around he gave her a ride home or arranged one, and Mama not even allowed to vote. One of the old women in Herrin did her the best turn: any time Mama wasn't going to make it out in time, she let her sleep over. The woman called them maid's quarters, nothing but a spare bed in her house. Mama said she just liked the company and used the ordinance as an excuse. Mama never got asked to stay at the Sneeds, just three doors down.

In his hurry to get out he'd left his jacket. Shelley lifted the summer wool to her nose and smelled cigar smoke and sweat. She slipped it on. The sleeves hung past her fingertips, and the hem came half to her knees. She felt the inside pockets and found his speech. She had to laugh. Thinking with the wrong head. Sort of sweet of him, in a way, giving up his power to her so easily. He was lonely. Not morose, though. He liked a good time. Hell yeah.

In the beginning Wallace had asked around, trying to be slick, but she'd heard and was able to arrange it quietly. She didn't blame him for wondering. Common whore wouldn't do. But damn. Now she was in the conspiracy that included his men (especially his own son-in-law— how did he handle *that*?), other miners who saw them together at the roadhouses, the families that the miners went home to, their friends, their phone friends, the mailmen, milkmen, slops men, icemen, and coal delivery men. All of Egypt put together was a small place when you looked at the size of its soul.

He *said* she didn't know. If it was the other way around, Shelley would have snatched him the rest of the way baldheaded just for putting her through something like that.

Shelley smiled. Who was she kidding? She too was in the center of a vast silence, just like Mrs. Sneed. Funny to think of her as that, but she did seem older than him. *You'd best never let her bring her white ass out here where I can get ahold of her.*

She heard the whistling and went ahead and opened the door a crack.

"He left in a hurry this morning," her brother said.

"Got a speech to make today," Shelley said. "Appears to be about those

59

scabs out at the Lester mine. Here, I assume you're going to the meeting. Take him his jacket, and for God's sake, get him his speech. Tell him I said nothing will win over the crowd better than killing 'em with kindness."

"You're in a good mood. Fixing breakfast?"

"Fix your own breakfast. Stove's lit."

Jeremy poured a little bacon fat into the skillet from the jar on the stove. When the tiny solids left from the bacon began to spit he cracked three eggs into the fat. Shelley sat on the bed reading the Bible.

"Jeremy, you know how you got to be a deputy?" she asked.

He shrugged, turned the eggs. "I asked Jimmy Hutcheons if I could be one. Waited 'til he was drunk. He about laughed himself inside out but said he'd think about it. Couple of weeks passed. I asked again, but he was sober that time. He said no, hell no, ain't never been no colored deputies, and he wasn't about to start any traditions. I said yeah but there's been coloreds run the fire brigade, and Paul Jackson was almost mayor and he's part colored. Hutcheons said No hell no. Then after a month he changed his mind. It's volunteer, anyhow. He's not out anything."

"Why did Hutcheons change his mind?"

"I don't know why the ignorant bastard does anything. He said nigras run fast—you know how he talks?—and if a thief needed catching when he didn't have any gas in his car, he'd wake me up."

"Jeremy, you ever think you'd get a real education?"

"What are you on about?"

"I don't know. Listen, Bill's been telling me about these places where we could go...."

"You and him?"

"You and me."

"He wants you gone? He must know you're in love with his big ass."

"Don't be ridiculous. Listen, in New Orleans, or New York, or Paris, we could work real work, and the people there wouldn't stand in the way. I could work and you could go to school. There are colored doctors, lawyers, even writers, Jeremy."

"Shut up."

"I'm serious."

"And you'd leave him just like that."

"Not just like that. He travels a lot. That's how he knows to tell me these things. He could catch up later."

"I don't get it," Jeremy said. He slid cut-up bits of egg white around in the yolk. "You were all in a panic, then you acted like you were sorry it didn't happen, and now you want to leave?"

"I don't know," Shelley said. "I just want you to do something more worthwhile than running errands. Nothing will ever change out here. I want to see you standing in a line, getting handed a diploma. And that music?" She hummed the opening to the graduation march everybody was using.

"Damn, boy, I can see you with a mortarboard on your head, and you're *strutting* up there to the head of the line." She put the Bible on her head and paced in a circle with her elbows out, pumping her fists like a drum major.

Jeremy laughed. "Crazy ass. I'll clean up later. I'm going out to the meeting now."

"You're sticking me with the cleaning, is what you're doing. Don't forget the jacket now. Just give it to him subtle."

"Okay, give it here."

"And mind you tell him the other thing I said. Forgot already, didn't you? Damn, Jeremy! 'Kill them with kindness.' That's what you're to tell him I said. And see what he does. I bet he busts up."

"I bet he doesn't, because I bet I don't do anything but give him his coat and leave. I'm not an errand boy," Jeremy said. "I'm a deputy sheriff, and don't you forget it." He stuck out his tongue at her on the way out.

She laughed and made a face. All of them were crazy as hell. About to fall together, colored and white, into the pit. Jeremy, so proud of that old tin-plate star with no power in it, not even a gun, just a way to make himself feel better for all he'd suffered. This she didn't understand. Jesus was the New Covenant. Faith in a future with old sins washed clean, that was what it meant to love. Hope for a new and better day.

She had suffered too, Lord knew *that*. Winters at twenty below, drifts four feet high against the house, and her as a little girl scavenging coal along the tracks to burn in that open grate in the one room. And in the summertime, helping Mama dig out some nasty bastard's outhouse because he was too cheap to dig another hole, scooping out the dried-up shit with shovels and then near the bottom where the shovel wouldn't work because the handle got in the way, using her hands. Dust everywhere and breathing in shit, lime, dirt. And after Mama died, those weeks in

Memphis and then East St. Louis. She thought she probably had a long list of people she could hate, most of them faceless and nameless. But making people anonymous was the way of darkness, and she chose light. Vengeance belonged to the Lord.

CHAPTER SIX

O'Rourke couldn't stand Malkovaich always hanging around his office, but he took a strange pride in Ol' Mal choosing his company, not the others'. For short periods it was interesting to hear Mal talk about the area—the big rivers that flowed together nearby, the dense forests of elm, hickory, and persimmon, the rolling hills filled with game. The problem was he never knew when to stop, and sometimes his droning filled the steel box for hours on end with no hope for O'Rourke's escape. He invented other places he had to be, only feet away, and managed to derail Mal temporarily. Unfortunately, the sliding door of the boxcar was rusted wide open, so he never had privacy. But it was nice, of a morning, when Mal was cooking, to sit alone in the shade at his desk and watch other men labor.

O'Rourke had already read all the other men's private files. They bored him since most were from Chicago too and their employment records showed they'd done little more with their lives than provide for their families. He wrote requests for sacks of beans and boxes of rivets that one of McDowell's men would buy in town. O'Rourke wanted to go along but McDowell said no. Night came, and he lay on his cot in the boxcar on the siding.

The next day was more of the same. The day after that he discovered he had piles.

A week dragged by like purgatory. Starved for excitement, he talked McDowell into sending a truck to an agricultural fair advertised in the paper. When they got to the grounds outside Marion, he shunned the other men from the mine and strolled alone, smiling. He held his breath through the sheep barn, stuck his finger surreptitiously in the prize-winning pie and licked it, and patted the neck of a horse with a braided mane. He let a carnie guess his weight (he was getting fat, as he suspected), tried his first cotton candy, and ate a pickle that burned from garlic with an Italian sausage fiery with spices. The whole time he pretended he was on a date. He and Mercy would pet the goats. He and Mercy would kiss in the funhouse and laugh at their shapes in the mirrors.

On the west edge of the fairground a band was playing popular tunes on a wagon decorated with bunting to look like a stage. A crowd had gathered and were tapping their feet and singing along:

Times are so bad and getting badder
Still we have fun
There's nothing surer
The rich get rich and the poor get laid off
In the meantime
In between time
Ain't we got fun.

O'Rourke, near the back, heard someone say the musicians aren't union and the whisper of the musicians aren't union went round that they weren't union as the singing tailed off because they weren't union musicians. Next thing somebody had pulled the chocks out from the wagon's wheels and two men with hard faces put their backs and legs into it, straining. The wagon began to roll down a low but steep hill and gained speed quickly. The men with banjos and clarinets were able to jump for it, but a scab drummer, a piano player and a bass fiddler, all trapped behind their instruments, were still aboard when the wagon burst through the tree line with one last angry, atonal chord, and the audience burst into applause.

O'Rourke decided from then on he'd stay at the mine, go through the motions of his days, and save his money for big things. His life was his to devise, and if he had to abide exile in a filthy coal mine in a rural backwater—probably called it Egypt because it was a gaunt-cow and swarm-of-locusts sort of place—then that is what he would do. The mine was nearly dead anyway, and O'Rourke loafed and smoked until called for meals.

To his surprise, Mercy replied to his letter. He thought less of her for that. He stood with her letter in his hand outside McDowell's office in the afternoon heat, afraid to open it, unsure how it had come to be. He was used to visiting his fantasies only on his own terms. In this way, he had a wealth of inner life but rarely compared it with reality so there could be no disappointment. He clambered into his office and read with utter delight. No one had ever cared to write him before. He read it again, again, and again. And again, laying it down and coming back to it more voraciously each time like a starving man finally provided bread. It was just as well it was only a paragraph long and mild since anything richer might have made him sick.

He knew he shouldn't reply right off, but he liked the image of being posted in a faraway land she was too innocent to know. He began to write back how the mine was embattled but realized he'd have to create details of a siege he'd never witnessed, so he tore up that draft and started another. Only as he was finishing it did he feel he'd gotten the tone right, so he ripped that letter up too and began a third.

In the next two weeks Mercy sent him three letters in all, and Jim studied them as carefully as an alienist might. He smelled them for any little whiff of her essence, held them to the light to see if traces of other writing had indented the paper—words to friends on how she really felt about him—and of course he read them a dozen or more times a day. Their content never varied, and he had memorized two of them—only a paragraph each—but it was her handwriting and his imagination that conspired to shift the meaning of certain passages every time he examined them. Had she written that line hastily, indicating she was going out to meet someone? Did the crabbed signature mean she was choked up with unspoken affection or did she want the letter—and him—done with as quickly as possible?

Jim admitted, after he spent himself, that Mercy was just the mildly interesting daughter of bourgeois, alarmingly religious parents who owned a little property but would never have cash. She was not beautiful. Neither the quantity nor the quality of her letters rivaled his, and she played at being older and noncommittal. Yet he ached and agonized over them, fondled, sniffed and tasted them as if they were women themselves, and while his separate peace lasted, he often lay face-down on his cot, staring furiously at one word left by her pen—"neighborhood," perhaps— and grinding himself into the canvas with his back bent painfully.

Malkovaich told him the trucks that re-supplied the mine had been parked permanently in a fenced lot in Marion so they couldn't be damaged by union men. Mal winked, and O'Rourke understood. Without trucks, there could be no work. Still, boredom was a sort of suffering.

There were ten heavily-armed guards then at the Lester mine. O'Rourke watched them talking in the boxcar they'd taken over for themselves. They took nearly as much mental energy as his obsessions with Mercy. He heard them bragging that they'd cut a road along the mine property with a steam shovel to keep union men from snooping too close and that farmers in the area were grousing about it. Then one morning Mal told him two of the guards had cursed and slapped a farmer who'd had a flat tire on a different road. These events were discussed in the camp, and the last two union miners working with special permission from their local left that day and never came back. The protests started that night.

A dozen men gathered in the dark around the mine and chanted something heard only as rhythms, they shot guns in the air and screamed, lit bonfires at a distance and danced around them like savages. They melted away before dawn.

O'Rourke had read about scenes like this in the Pennsylvania anthracite fields. He acknowledged the right of workers, just as he respected the great financiers' visions for the country, but the irrationality of the night worried him, and he slept less, staring blindly until he saw gray patches like ghosts and listening so carefully that his own breathing was painful to hear. He took more naps during the day to compensate.

One or more of the Chicago men fled the mine each night. In their haste they left behind their things, and McDowell told O'Rourke to inventory and catalog the personal effects as company property. Jim read the men's letters from home (boring), tried on their jackets (shoddily-made), and smoothed his hair with their hog-bristle brushes. He collected a small bag of the very best items to pawn in Chicago and kept this bag under his cot with a sheet over the bed that reached the floor.

Shortly after the protests began twenty-five new Pinks arrived. One afternoon they piled lazily from the truck and pulled weapons, boxes and duffle bags after them, looking more scrofulous than the original bunch if that was possible. O'Rourke peeked at them from the safety of his boxcar, tugged on the door again, and sat down out of their sight.

A cool breeze blew through his boxcar. The letter in the typewriter read, "June 15. Dearest Mercy,". The sun slanted in, warmed his back and lighted the mechanical guts of the typewriter before him on the desk. This *was* pretty country, he thought, especially when the sun was low on either horizon. Individual leaves of trees and bushes stood out sharply, and he could see the texture of shale far down the road where daisy-like flowers nodded in multitude. The land was different from anything he'd ever seen; Malkovaich said it was more Ozark Mountains than Illinois plains. The distinction seemed important, and it made him happy to share it with Mercy.

His goal was to have her welcome him back as a loved one, even though he'd left a stranger. The correspondence needed to progress in this vein. It had to work like a machine, step-by-step, leaving certain words standing out in the overall grid of the page to make the right impression.

The mine was an ugly goddamned place, after all, which most people, especially a beautiful young woman, would hate. But words like sunflowers, sunshine, and cool stream were cheerful, charming. Toads and daisies and soft rain would gain her confidence and make her sympathetic to him, then…. It was a hard life, and he deserved to have someone. He put his feet on his desk.

She would say to her parents mournfully over luncheon in their Winnetka summer home, My good friend Jim is serving in a place no man should have to live.

Is that the nice young man who came in the shop? the mother asked.

Dreadful, dreadful, what he must endure, said the father, who patterned himself on a Scottish country gentleman he'd read about in a novel. The deacons told me tales of Southern Illinois I'd never thought I would hear about in America. Of the English, perhaps. Wildmen and criminals. It's The South, of course, below Peoria. Unindustrialized, backward-thinking. But he's holding up? He tugged up his tartan trews.

Yes, he is, brave dear, and not a complaint to be found in his letters. I have to read between the lines to know at all what he's facing.

Well then, when your young adventurer returns from darkest Egypt we must have him to the house. He can stay with us as you become better acquainted.

Oh, *thank* you, Father.

According to the *Tribune*, the temperature in the city on June tenth had been a blustery 50 degrees. Even if he could get there (and he couldn't with the trucks behind a fence in Marion), Chicago's cold, high winds and frequent downpours made the beach, parks, carriage rides, and long walks he envisioned for them impossible. He sat with his hands in his lap. He wished he could bring Mercy here but her father, she indicated in a single line, was a dour Scots Presbyterian. It depressed Jim to realize that something as uncontrollable as the seasons—and the conditions of his employment—had conspired to keep him alone.

O'Rourke knew not to allow this into the letters. They were his envoys, they sat with her and courted her in his stead and lay next to her in the night. They should bring to mind lighter things. Magic and fairies, that's what women wanted. Sandstone formations in whimsical shapes— a camel, the Sphinx, Woodrow Wilson's face—silhouetted against the sky on bluffs in the heavily-wooded hills. The natives called that area Garden of the Gods. They also had a place they called Giant City, street-like paths among naturally-square sandstone boulders the size of houses, where Civil War deserters had hidden and scratched their names over ancient Indian drawings in the rock.

He would tell Mercy about the blackberries as big as quail eggs that grew wild along the dusty roads, about peach orchards heavy with fruit. He'd describe the taste of the cobblers the locals made of them, the smoked ham, dumplings, flour biscuits and jams. Delicious Italian pastas, salads, and bread, and Hungarian stews. Jim had never seen any of it, but Malkovaich had, and he could use it as a foundation to build his letters on.

He would describe to her a Sunday afternoon when a convoy of families drove past the mine on the way to a picnic and swim party. (Ol' Mal saw it happen once in the next county.) Or how some evenings at sunset a truck stopped in town on its way back from the Ohio River to sell channel cats and ancient-looking carp from dripping hoop barrels. (Mal said it was so.)

Mercy would share his delight in this and more. He would drive her in his Ford motor to the county seat to promenade the courthouse square and be seen by other young couples. They stopped at a store window to comment on the richness of the cloth. What a lovely dress. Well, you should know. Of course, silly, Father is a milliner, after all....

A man stepped into view, his head at knee-level. O'Rourke came to as if waking from a dream and felt a pang of shame at his longing.

"I say, old sport," the slightly younger man said. "Give us a hand, what? Me name's Prochnow, and I'm your new fraternity brother."

O'Rourke looked at him in disbelief. "What do you want?" he raged.

The man grinned. He scratched muttonchop sideburns with four fingers, carefully tickled the middle of his waxed mustache with a fingertip, then moved to the back of his head. O'Rourke heard his claws on his scalp, and the noise made him itch too.

"The bunkhouse is three cars back," O'Rourke said, still angry at being caught dreaming. "Go sleep with your own kind."

"I know where the bunkhouse is," Prochnow said. He spoke normally now, and O'Rourke thought he heard Chicago's South Side. "Bunkhouse is full. I'm sleeping here with you. Besides, there's some bad men in that lot. I'm skeered."

Prochnow threw a canvas bag up and slid a Winchester rifle onto the floor. A corrugated roof popped as it expanded, loud even over the grumble of steam shovels across the yard.

"What are you talking about?" O'Rourke whined. He felt the anonymity he'd been cultivating draining away. He'd begun to feel invisible and was a little surprised that Prochnow could find his car at all. "Go sleep in one of the admin buildings. I don't have room for you here." He knew by his sour stomach that Lester, or McDowell, or fate, had already decided against him long before he knew he'd lost.

Prochnow grinned and climbed into the car. "Aw, hell, Ethel," he said. "You have plenty of room. Besides, you might need me around later."

"Around for what?"

"Lester is shipping coal tomorrow morning. Why do you think he needs us Pinks? Say, how'd you get this far not knowing anything about American enterprise, old man?"

"I think I know a little something about the free market," O'Rourke sneered. "I've got investments."

"Yeah? Me too. Where's your money?"

"Where's *yours*?" O'Rourke said.

"Oh, Ethel. I'm so tired. Let me rest while it's still light out and then we can talk about where you hide your loot."

Prochnow stretched out between some filing cabinets, his head on his bag and rifle across his chest, and fell soundly asleep.

Well, O'Rourke thought. He didn't like this Ethel crap. He'd talk to McDowell *right* now and get this dolt out of here. He looked more closely at the sleeping man. His hair had been cut with a pocketknife, and he was dressed as a farmhand. But he was relatively clean. If he slept all day and stood guard at night, then O'Rourke could finally sleep. He slowly and quietly rolled the sheet of paper from the typewriter and hid it under a pile of requisition forms.

"What'd you do that for?" Prochnow asked from the floor.

"I thought you were asleep."

"I don't sleep. What'd you hide that paper for?"

"I'm not hiding anything."

"Yes, you are. Let's see. 'Dear Mercy.' That your woman?"

"A friend of mine."

"Ho ho. I'll bet."

"It's not really any of your concern."

"You're right there; no harm intended. So you write these women letters every day, do you?" Prochnow said.

"Not every day. And it's just one woman. My girl."

"Looks like you write her more than every day. Look at this pile of stuff."

"All that's not hers."

"What could you have to say that uses up so much paper?"

"We share things. What happens during the day. What we hope for the future. It's what people do, you know."

"Oh yeah? Does that work?"

"What do you mean, does it work? When I get home, we're going to do some of those things I write her about."

"Sex things? Do tell, Ethel."

O'Rourke blushed. "Don't you have somebody to write?"

Prochnow started as if he'd been lightly shocked. "What a great idea. I hadn't thought of it. I'm going to share some of that good stuff with one of my girlfriends back home."

O'Rourke grudgingly watched Prochnow roll a sheet of paper into his typewriter, but he couldn't help leaning in to see what he'd write.

"'Deer Sue,'" Prochnow typed, pecking pitifully at the keys with two fingers. "Crap, I messed that up. Hand me another sheet," he told

O'Rourke.

O'Rourke anxiously brought him half a ream of onionskin and set it on the table next to the typewriter. Prochnow hunted and pecked.

"Dear Sue, No dout you will be surprized to learn I am down here. With a gang of moonshiners ha ha. My gun fires quik as hell ands twice as mean. The muzzel velosty is 1000 yard a second and we got some here that does 6000 shots a piece. But as long as they stay 3 miles away they will be safe enough."

"You can't do that!" O'Rourke cried. "Move over. Get up, get up, here. I'll do it for you. You don't know anything about writing. Just tell me what you're trying to say, and I'll put it down for you. This is your girl?"

"One of many," Prochnow said. He flopped back on the floor with his back against his duffel bag and his hands cockily behind his head. "Boy, when I was your age, they called me Stiff Meat Henry."

"What the hell are you talking about?" O'Rourke said. "I'm older than you. Listen, what *doesn't* go in a letter, after muzzle velocities of weapons, is any mention of how she's not the only one for you. So: 'Dear Sue, You're the only thing I think about these days.' What else?"

"Tell her I can't wait to get back north."

"Good." O'Rourke typed something much longer. "What else?"

"Tell her I think how we met. How we started lovin' each other the second we was looking over them pictures in the museum."

"Really?" O'Rourke said.

"Oh yeah. Put all this down."

O'Rourke bent eagerly to the task.

"My darlin', we met in that big gallery, and you didn't care there were people everywhere or all that fancy art, and I pulled your shirt down hard over your titties and bit your nipples 'til you screamed out loud..."

"All right," O'Rourke said.

"...and you fell on your knees and sucked me so hard that in the end it was like a cannon going off my darlin' and your throat made a noise like a sewer drain: 'lo-lo-lo-lo-lo-lo.'"

O'Rourke was embarrassed at his tickle of arousal. "You're a cretin, Prochnow. You don't deserve a good woman."

"That's probably true," Prochnow said. "But turn 'em upside down and they all look alike anyway. My daddy always said that if they didn't

71

fuck there'd be a bounty on their heads. Listen, I'm just playing around with you. But if you're mailing your letter, would you mind posting something for me?"

He pulled clothing, books, a small box and a hatchet from his bag, and handed O'Rourke an envelope already sealed and stamped. The address read, "Mrs. Dean Prochnow, RR 2, Carrier Mills, Illinois."

"What is this?" O'Rourke said. "For your mother?"

"Nope."

"Your *wife*?" O'Rourke said. "Wait a minute. You're *from* here. Everything you just told me was a lie."

"I was just joshin' you. We got a good sense of humor down here."

Prochnow chanted in a sing-song voice: "We're the boys from Southern Illinoise, we live in caves and ditches. We beat our cocks on jagged rocks 'cause we're *mean* sons-a-bitches!"

O'Rourke felt a prickly panic-sweat emerge on his upper lip. Maybe, he thought, this was one of those striking miners in disguise. "What are you *doing* here?" he asked.

"Don't take it so hard, Ethel. Listen, I've been in the mines and the trenches, and broke horses, and laid track, and pinking is the best job I ever had. You sit around, eat good, draw good pay. I suspect you're here for some of the same reasons. But let's not kid ourselves. People outside this mine are going to try to kill us because they've had to do this hard damn work for forty years, and they'd like to do some more of it, at a fair wage, which I personally think should be as much as the market will bear. Here."

He handed O'Rourke a pistol from his bag.

"Take this barker. Won't do you much good, but it might make you feel better. Don't aim at their heads. I knew this guy got shot in the face and all it did was chip his teeth and make him meaner."

O'Rourke looked suspiciously at his hairy jowls.

"It's true, if you just wound somebody, it ties two of his buddies up 'cause they have to drag him off," Prochnow said. "If you kill him, they won't bother. But if I was you I'd aim for center anyway, heart and lungs, the ol' powerplant. Otherwise you take your chances."

"Look," he said kindly, seeing O'Rourke's distaste and fear. "Later I'll show you how to use the rifle too. You hit somebody with that and they stay down. Now I really do need to get some sleep. It's been a couple of days, boy."

When Prochnow was good and properly asleep, or appeared to be, O'Rourke sneaked out and hid the pistol in the tinderbox of the locomotive, thinking that getting it out of sight reduced the threat it represented. Then he put his letters and Prochnow's in the mailbag in McDowell's office. He imagined them speeding on their paths to those who, by their sex's sympathy and desirability, would save them from these silly games.

That night Prochnow woke him to point out a mass desertion, and O'Rourke took his turn watching men go through the open sights on Prochnow's rifle.

CHAPTER SEVEN

Bully caught a ride from the Crossing with other men headed for Reservoir Park. Most people curious enough to be there that Tuesday morning wouldn't be allowed in the meeting, but the park looked like a rollicking carnival when he arrived. He jumped from the truck as the driver looked for parking and a half-dozen other men shouted directions from the back. More than a hundred vehicles sat in the grass along the dirt track. Twice that many adults and children, many from neighboring counties, milled around chattering in the sun. More cars arrived, slowed to gawk and began to maneuver through the crowd. A drunk at the far end of the lines of parked vehicles helpfully waved newcomers to him, asking only, for his efforts, to be treated to a sip from their bottles. Sunnyside Mine was in the distance behind him.

The park surrounded a strip pit filled with rainwater, which everyone called a lake. Over the years it had been stocked with bluegill and catfish. Some of the crowd were already cooking what they'd caught, and Bully smelled smoking grease and hot cornbread. An old barn, separated into sweltering offices at ground level and a loft for assemblies, served as union hall.

Bully worked through the crowd toward the barn. Young women dressed in St. Louis fashions handed out chewing tobacco and cigarettes to anyone who wanted them, courtesy of Broad Leaf Tobacco, of Louisville, Kentucky. Bully took his share then two more shares when different girls came by. Boys watched the cigarette girls but lacked the nerve to chat them up, since the girls were older than the boys by two years and a world apart. Once he was in the shade Bully could see lovers entwined behind the great oaks, boys grinding girls into the bark with their passion. One of the girls pushed her boyfriend angrily and strode away. He followed, embarrassed to call out, and Bully laughed as the boy passed with his hard-on and upset red face.

Bullyrag nodded hello to men he knew. He was, after all, a miner in a crowd of miners, but his mine had only the one blaster, and he worked nights after the others quit for the day. In the past miners blew their own charges as they pleased and many died at once. This way, if something went wrong the company lost only one man.

Bully felt no obligation to stop at any one group. He'd played sports and hunted with them and used to arrive forty-five minutes early for work to change clothes and sit around in the bathhouse swapping lies. But that was before Sally.

He wished she were here now so they could squeeze hands or flick their eyes to point the other's attention. Despite their problems, Sally always knew why he looked at things. She's better than me, he thought. Well, smarter. At least more ambitious.

Three soapbox preachers had set themselves up within feet of each other and were trying to out-yell the competition. Their shouts jumbled with jeers and amens from the crowd, and each demanded the crowd listen to him and only to him, as he alone had the everlasting truth about the Love of Jesus Christ Our Lord and Savior, Lamb of Light, Bridegroom of the Soul.

On the west end of the park the husbands and wives whose children were grown and gone had planned ahead to be comfortable, packing chairs and zinc washtubs filled with ice and bottles of soda. A fiddler played "The Old Girl of Cairo Town" as a man and his rumpy wife swung around with linked arms. The man clogged a little then stopped to wipe sweat from his forehead. He turned to the others and said, "I've had it. Somebody else take her a while." His wife's heavy cheeks and chins bounced with her solo dance. The women had set out hot and cold dishes on a table spread with gingham cloth, and someone offered Bully a glass of iced tea with white sugar a half-inch deep on the bottom.

He kept walking. A woman stared at his hand; a man sized him up. He couldn't change their behavior, and it meant nothing. One old woman approached and began to harangue him on how this meeting would lead to no good, that Sneed was no good because he tried to appease rich people, what was needed was action. Bully walked past and the woman shifted her speech to someone standing nearby.

Behind the barn, Carl Shelton was drawing drafts from a keg in the back seat of his automobile. There was a line. Drinkers were forced to finish their beer where they stood and hand back the glasses before they could leave. A man that Bully thought had moved south a year ago poked Shelton in the arm. They looked up at him. Bully knew people associated him with Sneed, who to them was the law. Bully ignored them and pushed through a knot of men, women and children buying corn liquor from a woman who out-produced Sally, fifty-to-one, and had stills hidden in the woods from here to Mt. Vernon.

By ten a.m., many in the crowd had the slow movements and wise expressions of drinkers trying to hold on. One of them, Larry Jansen, stopped Bully and begged him to give Sneed a message.

"What makes you think I can tell him anything, or want to?" Bully said angrily.

"I want you to.... I put some of the best years of my life in those mines."

"That's what you want him to know?"

"No. I want to tell him I'm sorry I bothered Miz Sneed."

Bully held Jansen's shirt-front with his good hand and pushed him over, lowering him gently to the ground. "I'll tell him," Bully said. "Stay put."

Jansen appeared to consider, raised a finger to remind Bully of something, then relaxed. Rid of the contents of his mind and with Bully towering over him, he was free to pass out.

Most of the newsmen stood near the front doors to the Hall, smoking and joking. Bully knew Oldham Paisley and Hal Trovillion, who did nearly all the work of their papers themselves from writing to debt collection. He knew they struggled and put in hours, and people lauded them for that, but Bully always wanted to say in any case it wasn't mining. A reporter from the *St. Louis Globe-Democrat* was there and a small airplane had flown overhead, said to have been hired by a photographer from the *Chicago Tribune*. As Bullyrag passed the group Paisley reached out and caught his elbow.

"Mr. Greathouse, a word."

"What do you want?"

"I was wondering what you might tell us about the union's plans in this matter."

"How the hell should I know?" Bullyrag pulled away.

"But you are Mr. Sneed's brother-in-law, aren't you?"

Bully snorted.

"He mention anything to you or your wife that might indicate what he'll say in this meeting?"

"I think he'll say politicians are second only to reporters for being as useless as tits on a boar hog," Bully said. "Print that in your paper."

The newsmen chortled and talked quietly together. Fucking brute, one said.

Thinks if he's eccentric, nobody will bother him.

Too bad that hangfire didn't blow off that big head.

If he'd been hit in the head he wouldn't have been injured.

That's my point....

The point on the top of your head.

Looks like a horse, am I right? With that big head of his?

Probably hung like a horse too.

Yeah, said another and changed the subject. I'd rather eat a barrel of green worms than be married to that woman he's with.

Dust on the bust and coal in her hole.

You know that's not his wife.

What?

Not his wife. They were never married.

But they had a kid together. And they came from somewhere together, didn't they?

Her real name is Carmichael. I mean, it was Jones first, but then she married a man name of Carmichael. They were at Ludlow.

He was killed in the Ludlow Massacre? No wonder she's....

He wasn't killed. Ran off during the shooting, left ol' Sally hiding with the other wives and kids in a hole they dug under a tent. The Colorado National Guard and Rockefeller's men burned the camp down around them. The church wouldn't give her the divorce based on his cowardice, they said. I think she and this fella met in Chicago.

But he's from here, isn't he?

Carterville. Her too.

Of course, she and Sneed....

Adoptive. Personally I think she wants Sneed to meddle with her.

More likely she'd want to take charge, steal his vital essence, don't you know.

The only thing wrong with her is that she's like you, Hal: she wants to be thought of well by him. Equal footing. You guys are a democracy of three.

I thought she met Greathouse at one of those conventions.

She has been to those. She's friends with those Jews that sent that delegation.

What do you gotta be like that for?

What do you care? You one of her admirers, Oldham?

I'm saving myself for you.

The crowd grew noticeably louder when Sneed appeared at eleven. He motioned to union officials who rounded up their peers and selected miners, close to fifty in all. In solemn file, with Sneed at the head, they climbed a steep flight of stairs on the outside of the barn and disappeared into the converted loft. The crowd hushed watching them ascend. Bully waited until the last possible moment to make the climb. The stifling loft smelled of beer, sweat, and hay, and he pushed through bodies sitting on the floor and on benches to get to the back of the room.

The meeting had been called to order. A roll was being checked, but it took fifteen minutes to account for discrepancies. The men present looked at each other suspiciously, though they were all well known to one another. Only after Fox Hughes convinced himself there were no spies present did he order the minutes read. By the time the meeting proper began, the men had removed their jackets if they wore them, and Bullyrag's back was soaked with sweat.

Sneed began, telling them he would be brief. He looked tired and paced as if he was nervous or excited. His introduction reminded them that state senators, until 1913, had been chosen by state legislatures, and that he, by dint of representative democracy, was their true front man in all to come. He moved into the "equitable society" idea that Bully thought was fading and talked of unity in the face of absentee owners who would use machinery to double production and halve the workforce, the same heartless efficiency of the Great War, which many of those present had witnessed in all its carnage.

"By God, the government trained us to kill, I say we kill some scabs," a man near the front said.

"I used to pot Boche in the head from a hundred yards with an open-sight rifle," another man said. "I must have took out a thousand of those sumbitches." He guffawed, and his false teeth clacked.

Bully looked over at Michael Pape, a recent immigrant from the Harz Mountains. People said Pape's old father came into their yards and took chickens or pigs until somebody had to tell him America wasn't *that* free a country. Pape, it turned out, was an expert miner and had risen quickly in the ranks. He sat quietly in the corner.

"Gentlemen," Sneed said. "Please, just because you can do something doesn't mean you have to do it, or even that you *should*."

Hugh Willis stood and shouted, "Facts without force have never righted a single wrong!"

The volume began to rise.

"What the hell's that mean?" Bullyrag asked loudly from the back. His muscles tensed in an almost hysterical exhilaration and fear of public speaking.

"It means, Mr. Greathouse," Willis said with great dignity, "it means... well."

The assembly laughed heartily, and Sneed used the moment to regain control, winking at Bully to acknowledge the debt. He spoke then with great passion about the difficulties in the lives of all their families and called on individuals to testify. The performance seemed to be entirely off the cuff, and though Bully couldn't tell exactly what Sneed intended for them to do—especially in this business about public opinion and the law—he felt as if something had been decided.

Bully wondered how men like him did it. Did they stay up all night, memorizing everything including possible sidebars? Or was it a trick, where well-worn phrases stood in for original ideas? In any case, Bully could see by the tight pride on Sneed's face that he knew he was doing the thing. Bully looked away so as not to distract him and so he wouldn't have to see it in his eyes.

Bully hated crowds, being in crowds, being seen by crowds, and he had once told Sally that a congregation of more than three was a mob. She had thought and said seriously, "Maybe that's why our baby died, Bully. We're such different people: I organize, you elude."

It led to an epic argument that drove their neighbors out of their own homes in embarrassment, but Bully hadn't hit her even when she hit him first, and her breaking her nose later that afternoon with the door was an accident not at all related to the fight really.

The day was more brilliant when the delegates emerged. The air felt cool after two hours in the loft, but the overhead sun had been particularly bad for the drunks outside, whose scalps were pink and growing tender. At first Bully didn't recognize anyone and wondered if rabble-rousers had driven away the old couples and young lovers. Sneed told everyone to go on home and left himself.

Men began to come together in twos and threes to grumble and chew the fat. After a while, one or two shoved the preachers off their boxes and shouted for justice. Dozens of men gathered to listen, their women retreating a safe distance to mutter behind their hands. The remaining older folks got tired of the foul language and rudeness, as did the families, who didn't want their children to hear about violence in a public venue, even if they condoned it. Some teenage couples departed in search of privacy, others from boredom. But the party was over, and those who had driven far on poor roads wanted something for their time. Bullyrag walked around and listened, thinking Sally was still a better speaker.

A car arrived from town with stacks of the latest edition of the *Herrin News*. There weren't enough copies to go around, and some, including Bully, had to have it read to them, but within minutes everyone was clear on what had happened.

The front page showed two telegrams, side-by-side. One was Sneed's telegram to John Lewis of the day before. The other was Lewis' reply:

Cincinnati, June 19, 1922
Wm. J. Sneed, President Sub-District 12,
UMW of A, Herrin, Ill.

In reply to your wire of today. Steam Shovelers Union was suspended from affiliation with American Federation of Labor some years ago. It was also ordered suspended from the mining department of the A.F. of L. at the Atlantic City Convention. We now find that this outlaw organization is permitting its members to act as strike breakers at strip mines in Ohio. This organization is furnishing steam shovel engineers to work under armed guards with strike breakers. It is not true that any form of agreement exists by and between this organization and the mining department or any other branch of the A.F. of L. permitting them to work under such circumstances. We have thru representatives officially taken this question up with the officers of the Steam Shovelers Union and have failed to secure any satisfaction. Representatives of our organization are justified in treating this crowd as an outlaw organization and in viewing its members in the same light as they do any other common strikebreakers.

(Signed) JOHN L. LEWIS

This was the satisfaction the crowd had been waiting for. A yawp rose from the park, loud enough for the old man guarding the closed Sunnyside mine office to look down the road in apprehension. He was paid to keep the fire going under the steam boiler twenty-four hours so the pumps kept working and the mine didn't flood, and he knew his constant paycheck was a goad to the unemployed. Men raced the engines on their trucks, backed them, jolted forward again in three-point turns, and narrowly missing one another, sped away with passengers still clambering from bumpers to beds, running boards to cabs.

Soon Bully was the only one upright in the park. Five men, a woman and two boys lay in more or less advantageous places to be passed out. He walked around, pulled a boy back from the edge of the reservoir and picked up a bottle of red wine that lay forgotten in the grass. With the little finger on his mutilated hand, he pushed the cork down into the bottle. He sat heavily and turned the bottle up and drank. Sally, he knew, was going to be interested in this, and he felt the wine warm his stomach as he lay in the sun and anticipated bringing the scene home to her. But after another long pull he felt silly for thinking like a boy with a happy report card, and he determined to stay out even longer. He'd stay out until Sally would have to wonder if he was okay. He wanted her to want to know where he was, which she never did, as if she didn't care or didn't think he had it in him to be bad. He just didn't want her to nag him about it.

Things weren't as good as they had once been. But Bully's emotional life lay in the memory-shadow of seeing her come around to him, admire him, show respect. When *she'd* suggested sleeping together—good god, what a feeling. He'd grinned and said he'd have to take her up on that offer or else stick his head under the wheel of a passing truck for being a goddamn fool. Then they got serious and loving, and it had stayed that way a good long time.

There were still some fine times. He wished she wasn't holding her own meeting now so he could be the one to walk in on her instead of the other way around. He was bored to death but stayed and stayed at the reservoir and took the long way home to kill even more time, but on his arrival the house was empty, and it hurt not to be able to hold his little boy.

CHAPTER EIGHT

Cora was having a bad day, and none of it, she thought, was her fault. One could not exaggerate the strain of living in another's shadow. Will's comings and goings had interrupted her all morning, and it wasn't just his appearing and disappearing with little more than a word for her and the children these days. It was his sudden turns of mood, jubilant yesterday after he came home from his speech, in a panicked frenzy today over where to hide the guns.

Used to be, when he spent weeks at a time away, he was able to separate the two aspects of his life, so when he was home he was home—no sullen silences or retreats to unoccupied rooms. Maybe she was to blame, Cora thought. But he couldn't seem to make himself happy, and if she were the cause of it, he would have gotten rid of her somehow. Men wouldn't live in constant unhappiness. It just wasn't their nature.

There was a moment in her life. It had passed now of course, and she couldn't even say when. But one more infinitesimal weight dropped, the scales tipped, and she was certain against hope that she would always face disappointment. She had awakened to fatigue, loneliness, and the realization she wasn't as good as those who came before. Her life with Will and the children was fine. But the other thing hurt and even if it was fairly mild it was always. Since then it had worn her down, and she was afraid it would win entirely before she died, leaving her crippled and disfigured.

This morning Will had been tired but eager to get going. He assured her everything was fine but had told the help to stay home. Cora knew full well how to fry a slice of ham and cook his eggs over runny as he called them and make red-eye from the grease. She poured coffee. Will was dressed in his darkest and most authoritative suit.

"I'm very proud of you," Cora said.

Will grinned at her the way he used to, close to forty but just a kid. "Really, Tooks?" he said. "How proud?"

"Enough to bust all my buttons." She put her arms around his neck.

Will hugged her so she could barely breathe. "Cora, you are sweeter than pecan pie," he said. "Love you."

"Love you too," she said.

He told her he had meetings all day but would check in periodically and if Sheriff Thaxton called to tell him to stay put at a phone because Will wanted to speak to him.

Cora went about the chores herself. It was hard, with the baby especially, and her body hurt in places the young didn't feel. She put Helen in to play with Marjorie in her room, made the older girl swear to come get her if there was a problem, and went downstairs. She heated the sad irons on the stove and cleared the kitchen table and covered it with an old sheet. No one came begging at the door to interrupt. She washed a week's worth of shirts, pushed them through the wringer and was hanging them on the line when the phone rang. It was one of the first phones in town and made the outdated rumbling jingle that could be heard several houses away. Old man Henderson and his young wife looked out their side window. Lena House waved at Cora from her own backyard. She too was hanging clothes.

"Your phone," Lena said. "Maybe it's Will."

"I've got it," Cora called. Lord, as if she needed the neighborhood to tell her to answer her own phone.

Will said, "Cora, I need you to look in my book for a number."

She left the phone hanging and went to the kitchen counter near the back door where he usually kept the book. It wasn't there.

"It wasn't there," she said.

"You must find it. Go look in my study."

Cora found the address book half-buried in papers on Will's desk. As she pulled the book from under them she caught a glimpse of the pistol.

"What were you thinking?" she said to him. "How could you? With children in the house? I won't have it."

"Throw it out, then, I don't care."

"I won't touch that thing."

84

"Fine, then leave it. I'll throw it out myself. Just give me the number."

"Wait. I'm looking." She scanned each entry quickly for names she didn't recognize. "What in the world did you bring it here for in the first place?"

"Lord God, Cora. There's no time. They're talking about calling in three companies of the National Guard. Give me the goddamn number."

"Okay, Will, don't be cross."

"Keep your priorities straight. I'll explain everything later, when there's time. Why would you think there's time for all that now? I called you with an important request. Just one request...."

"Okay, Will, stop it. Be quiet. Here's the number."

Cora just managed to feed the girls before the phone rang again.

"Thaxton?" Will asked without saying hello.

"No. Are things going well?"

"It's unbelievable."

"Good news?"

"Of course not. What do you think? Some of our men may have ambushed a truckload of nonunion men coming in from Carbondale. Sounds like they managed to kill some."

"Oh, Will. It's happening."

"No, no, don't jump to conclusions, Cora. Everything will be fine. Don't worry yourself. I'm going out to Carterville to see what's happened."

"Please don't. Come home now."

"I'll be home shortly."

Cora turned to see Lena House and two other neighbor women standing outside the screen door.

"What is it?" they asked.

"You might as well come in," Cora said. She made tea, and the women took turns listening to the phone. It was a party line, and the news had begun to spread. Several hundred men from the area were gathered in the Herrin Cemetery for what they called an indignation meeting. Will's telegram and Lewis' reply had been read and discussed.

"Oh Lord," Lena said. "Men without regular jobs are hazards."

They sat in the kitchen and listened. The heat from the cookstove made it uncomfortable, but none of them suggested they go elsewhere.

The clock ticked, the house creaked as it settled, children pulled a wagon over the brick street. Then, like a storm building, the sound of motors began to grow on Park Avenue. Cars and trucks, a few at first, then more, raced past the house. Men's voices called to each other over the noise, loud but unintelligible. None of the women wanted to be without a phone, so they left Cora and went home.

She was mesmerized by the flow of traffic like a river and felt the excitement in it as it ran, and she hadn't given a thought to any of the cars stopping. Then the Lincoln pulled into the drive, and she saw Will in the backseat, waving his hand at Wallace to put the car behind the house. She was curious why he parked so far in back.

She waited by the front door for him to enter as he always did. Instead, the back screen flew open suddenly against the squawk of its spring and hit the side of the house, startling her. She walked back through the house to the kitchen. Will stood just inside the door. Wallace was behind him, his arms filled with rifles of different lengths and shapes as if they were a bouquet of flowers, and he looked sheepish as he stepped inside.

"Didn't see a mat to wipe my feet, Mother Sneed," he said.

"No," Cora said. "No more guns."

"Are you crazy?" Will said. "They're looting the hardware stores, demanding to borrow all the guns and ammunition. The American Legion Hall was nearly broken into for the parade rifles. Wallace and I confiscated what we could. There's more in the car."

"Ruby's safe, Mother," Wallace said, the bouquet of guns held foolishly in his arms. "I checked on her and she's safe at home."

"You cannot put these weapons in our home," Cora cried. "Think of the baby."

Will paused, a half-step falter, then threw rifles with a clatter on the divan in the next room.

"I don't have any other option, Cora." He stopped and looked out the front-room window. Cars scuttled across the lenses in his glasses like ghosts. "We've lost control. Many of them are ours," he said, pointing. "Most."

Cora shrank from him. "Where are you going to hide these things?"

"Hide?"

"I won't have guns lying around my house. What if Helen gets into them?"

"Right," Will said. "I'll lock them up. Where?" he asked, as if Cora should have the answer.

There were so many weapons, dozens, that the only thing to do was put them in the basement. Will told Wallace to hide them under the coal in the bin then said forget it, there wasn't time, just throw them in, let's go. They climbed the stairs, and he closed the door to the cellar and had Wallace hammer twenty-penny spikes through the door into the frame.

"Stay inside, keep the children with you," Will said as they left.

Cora was so angry she swept the entryway with a broom reserved for the porch. She jabbed under a table, and a vase fell to the floor without breaking. Cora began to cry and quickly built to a burning, swollen-eyed sobbing that made her chest spasm with the effort. Yet something very hard inside watched and asked if she had ever acted this way before. She had, one day ten years after the death of her ungrieved father, when she spent two hours sobbing behind a leather chair that had belonged to him. And now as she struggled for breath she thought how good it felt to have something all hers, even misery. No, she remembered, the children belonged to her and no other.

Cora determined to hold the routine of the house together no matter what happened in the world outside. She put the children in the playroom with lunch. Then she sprinkled several shirts with starch water and ironed them, alternating the two irons heating on the stovetop. The comforting smell of the starch rose in the steam, and her bare feet stuck to the linoleum. She wondered what her life might have been like if not spent with Will. His bullheadedness, crabbiness, insults, the labor problems. She had been the daughter of a merchant and had lowered herself to be the wife of a miner. But then he became a politician entrenched in difficult issues, and that was an awkward and tenuous gain.

She guessed now that her dreams had been East Coast dreams, salons, gentle and cultured ladies and gentlemen who, between dinner and supper, took expeditions to the zoo or went ice-skating. That was her idea of adventure in those days, and she had lulled herself to sleep with those daydreams nearly every night of her youth. She didn't do that anymore.

She would like someone to tell her she was beautiful, to have Will think so. Sagging belly and lopsided breasts after the children, the dark veins under her pale skin like the tributaries of a river. And what good would it do to be beautiful? Will could simply live with her as plain old mortals do, not always be straining, straining, to be something he wasn't, always thinking of others before his own kin. Forcing her to play Rubber bridge with the wives of the lumber-company owner and the vice-president at the bank. She could have had the kind of life where she was able to wear nice clothes and hear elegant people small-talk and see them smile at her entrance. Bob her hair, buy ribbons. She felt like crying again at her own pitiful....

Someone knocked lightly with a knuckle, *tap-tap*, on the front screen door. The main door stood open for the air. Cora froze. The knock grew louder, bolder. The hobos knew to come to the back door. They had their marks scratched into her fence and trees. She was angry but automatically thought of what she had in the house to feed him as she went.

A man she had seen somewhere—he was dressed in miner's coveralls and boots, so who knew?—turned from the door as he saw her coming and stepped off the porch. Cora saw more men in the yard, facing her as if she was about to come on stage from the wings.

She knew none of her upset must show now or it would all be gone, swept away like wrack in a flood. Strangers in their house, kidnapped children, rape, ransacking, theft, the house burned to the ground. Her mind accepted the danger and something changed in her body as she went forward, tempered like steel. She slipped the catch on the screen and stepped outside.

"Yes? What is it?" she said. She stood up straight and held her hands together at the waist.

There were eight of them, or so she guessed later when she tried to remember. The scene was before her as she stood on the porch, but she couldn't see any of them clearly or count their number. The miners seemed strangely uncomfortable freed from the blackness of the mine and were sober, purposeful, and happy only to the degree that they could play at being courtly. First one and then the others removed their hats.

"Miz Sneed, we come for the guns," a man said. He was the one who had knocked, and he stood a step or two closer than the rest.

"You're Jansen, aren't you?" she said. "I recognize you from before."

"Yes, ma'am. You have been kind enough in the past to afford me something from your larder when I needed a little something to get by." He looked left and right at the other men and stepped another step closer.

"Miz Sneed, now we know Mr. Sneed took some guns that are rightfully ours. And we come to claim them. It ain't right he tells us we're to do a thing and then tries to stop us from doing it."

"There are no guns in this house," Cora said. "Please leave my yard immediately."

"We know there is guns here, Miz Sneed. We ain't causing you no harm by asking for them, am I right?"

"It's no harm to ask. And now you've asked and had an answer. Good day."

"Miz Sneed. Ain't right a lady like you lying to us. We're just dumb working men, but we know better than that."

"Men, you know the power my husband holds here. Must I call the police?"

Jansen snickered. "The police got their hands in their pockets. They're downtown watching us arm ourselves. Some have even said they'll join us when their shift's over."

"Nevertheless. My husband...."

"Mr. Sneed said we could come and get them, ma'am," a man on her left called. "Really, he did. Call him if you'd like. I believe he's down to the union hall."

Cora felt their lies eroding her resolve. She had expected the violence instantly if it was to come, not after protracted negotiation. She smiled painfully at the men.

"Very well, gentlemen. I will call Senator Sneed, and if I cannot reach him, I will take your word that he intended for you to have some guns, which honestly I don't know about. In that case you will have to help me search for them. If they are in the attic, I don't want to get myself dirty, so I'll have to ask you to get them yourselves." She smiled again.

"Oh yes ma'am."

"Stay here." The iron will was back, and she held them in her blind gaze. The world spun and sunlight flared. After the pause that reminded them she was no one to disobey, she went inside, dizzy with panic.

If she gave them what they wanted she could think of three bad results, and she thought of them in no particular order: Will would be mad; the men would kill her and the children anyway; and someone else would die as a result of her cowardice. She walked back to the phone mounted on the wall and turned the crank a couple of times so they would think she was placing the call. She wished now she could get to the guns herself. Not that she knew how to use one, but she'd seen pictures of doughboys raising them to their shoulders.

She realized she couldn't be seen if she stayed in the back of the house, nor heard if she had no shoes. She cut through the kitchen and the hot room for winter laundry then came up the hallway in back and into Will's study, as if his presence was stronger there than anywhere else in the house.

When she opened the front screen door again, quickly, she'd been gone less than a minute but already Larry Jansen had one foot on the top step to her porch and was quietly demanding the others follow. He half-turned and saw her coming at him rapidly in her black dress, cameo on her breast, hair severe, and feet white and bare as a corpse's. Jansen leaned back and missed the next step, ran backward off-balance and fell on his rear with a grunt at the feet of one of the other men.

"How *dare* you come to *my* house and make demands," Cora hissed. "How dare you sully my porch with your filthy feet and murderous intent, and after I *fed* you as if you were one of my own."

"Now Miz Sneed," Jansen wheedled from the ground. "We are your boys," he said, indicating the worn, middle-aged miners around him. "And we would never do anything to you or anything to upset Mr. Sneed. He's one of us in this thing."

"He represents you, you ass, in what should be the noblest struggle of our time, and you will never mention his name again in conjunction with any of your pursuits, I'll bet you that." Her voice had gotten quieter as she got madder.

"Miz Sneed," Jansen said, grinning now and advancing, evidently mistaking her quiet for helplessness.

Cora pointed Will's old pistol into the air over Jansen's head and pulled the trigger. The hammer rose and fell on a dead cartridge. She didn't know what it meant that there had been no explosion. But the men in the yard had ducked when she brandished the gun. The sight of them was hilarious. She felt like laughing at the fools. She didn't laugh because she knew she had lost.

All the men stepped forward slowly now, not rushing her, she knew, because they believed they'd simply walk into her house. The blurred forms and soft march of their boots on the grass overwhelmed, and as the mass of denim, leather, and flesh closed, she pointed Will's pistol directly into its collective face and fired.

The bullet ripped off the lobe of Jansen's right ear and drilled into the lawn; powder stung the faces of three others. They jerked back again, sure they were shot this time. Jansen was the only one still upright, and he grinned stupidly as blood ran down his neck and onto his shoulder. The others froze in half-crouches with their arms over their ears like giant fetuses.

She thought she'd killed them, and it was liberating to take charge of a power this malevolent in her bare feet on her own porch. When she saw they weren't even seriously wounded, as if she had known what she was doing with the pistol, like some trick-shooting Annie Oakley, it felt even better, and she laughed.

"Now get off my property," she said. "And I will personally see to it that Mr. Sneed deals with each and every one of you in turn."

The men gaped, looked at each other, backed away.

"No one dare threaten me and my children in my home!" Cora's voice raised. "I'll tell Will every one of your names," she said and felt the joy of righteous anger coming over her. When she saw her words had an effect—the men began to dogtrot down the street—her rage blossomed fully. "I'll kill you! I will kill you all!" she screamed and shook the pistol at them as if it was an extension of her finger.

For several minutes the memory of the scene continued to build within her as she paced the house and spoke her lines out loud, thought of new and better ones, laughed, and sighted down the barrel of the pistol at the things of her home, until she began to think she'd lost her mind. She even yelled unwittingly at the neighbors, including cousin Lena, and helpful Mr. Van Buren, to stay out of her yard. But Marjorie stuck her head around the banister and said, "Mama?" in a scared voice and began to cry when she saw it was all right and that broke the spell. Cora calmed herself and invited the neighbors in. Lena made tea and buttered bread for them while they all discussed what to do. Each gave a tug at the cellar door but it wouldn't give. Van Buren offered to get a crowbar but Cora asked if that would damage the door and when he said it probably would she stopped him.

While the tea steeped the little group walked around the house and peered into the cellar through the windows. Everyone agreed that no one but a child could crawl in through the tiny windows, and Cora, back in charge, would not allow any of their children to do so. Finally she herself slid down the coal chute, clawed and pushed her way through the small mountain of nut coal in the bin that Will got for free, and handed rifles through the window for everyone, choosing the biggest, most impressive-looking ones, and all the boxes of cartridges she found. Mr. Van Buren showed them how to load the guns with the correct size ammunition.

"Imagine," Cora said, laughing, "I had no idea they made different-sized bullets."

Cora, Lena House, Old Man Henderson and his wife, and Mr. Van Buren sat in the parlor and drank their tea with rifles balanced on their laps. A pair of cardinals sang outside, and Cora smelled dust in the curtains warming in the sun. She'd have to beat them soon, and the rugs too. And of course her clothing was ruined with coal dust along with the towels they were all sitting on. Coal was awful, filthy, oily stuff. Even the word was bad. *Coal.* It was as bad as "Labor," or "Capital," or "industrial conflict." But the tea was perfectly lovely. Everyone agreed they would like more so Lena heated more water to top up the pot.

When Will finally appeared, close to what should have been a normal suppertime, though no supper had been prepared or even discussed yet, he was walking, down at the mouth, and he barely greeted the neighbors when he came in. They sensed more trouble, so they stacked their rifles in a corner, efficiently and soldierly, and went home.

"They stole the car," Will told Cora. "I went in to talk sense to a bunch that were getting ready to tear down Smith Hardware. Jim wouldn't give them guns on credit, and they would have killed him over it. Wallace got pulled out of the car and was kicked in the face. Probably broke his nose. Worse, the bastards have my car."

"Who cares about the car?" Cora said. "They were here too."

As if just noticing the rifles freed from the cellar Will said, "The children?" He looked at her dirty face and loose strands of hair.

"Fine, Will. But Larry Jansen...." She couldn't finish and began to laugh, much to Will's displeasure. The disapproval on his face only made her laugh harder though it didn't feel much like laughter anymore. He held her upper arms as if to comfort her but shook her hard a couple of times instead and she began to cry. She told him the story then and begged to know what they'd do. Will ignored her and went to check on his daughters.

When he returned Cora was sober again. He belabored the situation with the car until she said, "Who cares about the goddamned car? What about our family?"

Will was shocked. She'd never cursed in twenty years of marriage and in fact she'd always been on him that if he couldn't say something without foul language, he didn't know enough to open his mouth. There'd been plenty he'd started to say around her but didn't finish.

Now he said, "I don't care about that car any more than you do. Probably less. But it has my senate star on its grill and my congressional plates, front and back. People will think it's me inside or that I've authorized them to use it. Who will stop them in anything they do? I'm ruined."

Chapter Nine

Prochnow was awake and potential entertainment, and O'Rourke, who'd eaten several dinners through the course of the afternoon, was overstuffed and bored.

"So who do you know that was shot in the mouth?" he asked.

"Now this here is what we call a licorice stick. Dynamite," Prochnow said, ignoring him, lifting a stick from others that lay like cigars in a wooden box.

"I know what dynamite is," O'Rourke said. He was too terrified to move at the sight of it, and his instant rage at being made a victim again froze inside, where it worked jaggedly in his gut and made him deeply nauseous.

"And this," Prochnow said, still ignoring him as he pulled a small metal tube from a separate bag, "is a blasting cap. Never keep the two together in one place. See, dynamite, unless it gets old and the nitro starts to sweat out of it, is pretty stable."

He knocked the end of the stick of dynamite against O'Rourke's desk. O'Rourke's breath stopped.

"But caps will go off pretty easy. So you want to keep your primary charge, the cap, separate from the secondary charge, the dynamite stick. That way, when you fall ass over teakettle and your cap explodes, you don't get blown sky-high by the dynamite."

He gave O'Rourke a blasting cap and a length of fuse.

"Put the time fuse in the end of the cap. Then you'll need to crimp the cap to the fuse."

O'Rourke was shaking at the concentrated power like fate in his hands.

"Put the fuse in like this?"

"That's right. Now you need to crimp it so it stays there. Put the cap between your teeth and bite down on it so the edges of the tin crimp to the fuse."

"You say to put it in my mouth?"

"Right."

"Like this?"

"That's right. Not so tight."

"Sorry."

"Now put it in further. There. And bite. Hard. Harder."

"Like this?"

"Yes."

"Oh."

"How's that feel?"

"Good. But if blasting caps are so touchy, won't it go off when I bite down?"

"Oh god yeah," Prochnow said. "Lots of guys get their noses, tongues, lips blown off that way. We call them Grinning Gusses, 'cause there's nothing left to their face but a big smile from their eyeballs down to their chins. We also call them stupid bastards. So you don't want to do it that way."

O'Rourke pulled the cap from between his teeth, horrified.

Prochnow showed O'Rourke what looked like a pair of pliers. "Crimping tool," he said. "I use it to put everything together. Fuse in the cap, cap in here, then hold the whole thing behind you and squeeze it tight. This way, if it goes off, you just get shrapnel in your ass."

"You let me bite down on that? I could have killed myself!"

Prochnow looked amused. "Probably not. Look, Ethel, it's more forgiving than most people are."

He held up his primed explosive by the fuse and began to sing a tuneless song, acting it out as he sang: "You can shake it..."

He shook the dynamite heartily.

"...you can swing it..."

He twirled it in tight circles by its fuse.

"...you can bang it; you can bounce it, you can toss it...."

He threw it to O'Rourke and laughed delightedly at his terror dance.

95

"You're all right, Ethel," he said. "I don't care what the other Pinks say about you. There's one over there that's got it in for you. Former federal lawman name of Glenn. Says you remind him of somebody. His wife. And he *hates* his wife."

O'Rourke knew the bit about the other mine guards was a joke, and he liked Prochnow. There was something trustworthy about someone who knew violence professionally. After supper and several hands of cards in the light summer evening, in which he took three dollars from Prochnow, O'Rourke considered him as good a friend as he'd ever had and silently counted on him to take part in some future, undetermined caper. They turned out the lantern as soon as it was fully dark out so the bugs wouldn't gather, and while Prochnow stood watch, O'Rourke tried to fall sleep.

Now the mine was officially locked down—no one in, no one out. Malkovaich had told him deserters would be shot by the Pinkertons. O'Rourke didn't believe it. They were accountants and cooks, for Christ's sake. His indignation rose at being held captive, whether by Pinks or by rogue forces outside the mine. Anybody who tried to keep you back from what you wanted was evil.

Besides, he'd heard no shots within the perimeter, and men had escaped. He determined to pack two canvas bags with his clothes and the personal effects of those who defected before him, lace his boots up tight with his paychecks safe in his socks, and walk down the dirt road past the slag heaps through the wild carrots to the paved road that led to the highway. He'd thumb a ride with a passing farmer and leave this place forever. He would do it. Today. This very night.

Then again Malkovaich had fought in the war and wouldn't be prone to exaggeration. O'Rourke stifled an urge to call into the darkness and ask Prochnow outright what he would do but the thought was ridiculous and paranoid, and he didn't want to put any ideas in his head. He wasn't too bright, maybe even a little retarded. O'Rourke wasn't sure Prochnow wouldn't wound him merely as a joke.

What really got O'Rourke was that these were *Americans* on both sides of this thing. In Chicago the constant waves of newcomers made it hard to tell who belonged sometimes, but he was pretty sure it was foreigners causing most of the trouble. O'Rourke hated the Irish who were always trying to remake Cook County into County Dingle. He had no interest in the Uprisings or the Black and Tans or the Old Sod or anything else of that sort. His break with ethnicity and politics had been so complete that he marveled at why people got involved in, let alone killed over, such issues.

To be an American was to do American things: to build a decent life on American soil, to accumulate wealth, to fight and die if necessary to protect American interests, though he himself had found a way around that during the war.

He didn't give a tuppeny damn where his parents came from. They'd never done anything for him but leave him like baggage with a great-uncle one night when he had a toothache and never came back to collect him. The old man hadn't lasted long and then there was the orphanage, the whorehouse, the street. More recently that awful ship for two weeks and the naval pie-wagon for running off when they pulled into Norfolk. What the hell did he care about other people's ideas of dishonor?

Life was too hard to worry about what somebody else thought: eating the dirt of Little Egypt with every meal, earning lousy pay, mining coal, being apart from quality people such as Mercy and her family. He wondered if she had siblings. Brothers could be a problem but sisters would be fine. But here he was, stuck with hard men and hard goddamn luck. The future would begin the second he got on the back of a truck and left this god-forsaken hole in the ground with its various tyrants inside and out.

He imagined himself invisible and able to fly at great speeds. In his drowsing dream he flew out of rocky Southern Illinois, sped over the soft prairies of midstate and went directly to the swankiest hotel he'd ever seen in person, The Drake. He floated past the doormen in their rich brocades and red caps and over ladies taking cream tea, squeezed into the elevator as it was closing and lay on the couch. The operator took a couple to the fourth floor. They turned to the right; he drifted down the hallway to the left, trying doorknobs, until he found an open suite. Without disturbing the occupants asleep in their bed, he curled like a puppy in a corner. It was dark. He was safe. The room smelled of starched sheets and perfume.

He stretched on his cot, aware he could drink their whiskey, pilfer a pocketbook, eat leftover grub from the room service cart. Ducky.

Or he could pull down the blanket, gently untie the lady's night-gown.... O'Rourke's idea seemed to waken her lover who raised to an elbow and began to kiss her neck. She made a small noise as Prochnow pulled her gown down over her breasts more roughly. The moonlight pierced the drapes and revealed the enlarged pores around Mercy's large pink aureoles.

O'Rourke woke with a start, jealous and angry, remembering the musk and slap that should have been his, his erection bent painfully under him. Prochnow was asleep, and O'Rourke thought of how everybody he'd ever known had done him dirty. He masturbated as efficiently as an accountant, with a minimum of motion and effort, so Prochnow wouldn't hear. He didn't know what to do with the jism in his palm so he ate it and fell soundly asleep.

The next morning after his usual breakfast of eggs, bacon, biscuits, gravy, grits with sugar and cream, and coffee, he sat down to write a letter to Mercy but the edge was off his longing. Prochnow was still asleep or pretended to be. He twisted the knob on the typewriter and the blank white paper moved up and down in the rollers. If he caught a train he could be with Mercy in just four hours. Prochnow stirred and stretched, and O'Rourke looked at him hopefully. Prochnow grunted, farted a blast like Gabriel's trumpet and went back to sleep.

O'Rourke's spirits sank rapidly. There was no greater distance than time. Right now was right now, and Mercy was far far away. He might as well be the man on the moon.

He forgot about Mercy's letter as his vague image of her got mixed up with his vague idea of the good life. Comfort, peace, no more scams and scrambling. A home, something permanent this time. He would share it but had to get it the way he wanted it first. He mentally listed the things he would buy a woman after he established himself—French perfume, a mink stole, opera tickets, silverware in a wooden case, fine china in a hutch the length of a wall, another cabinet for porcelain curios. He would take her on the train to the Indiana Dunes or up to northern Wisconsin for weekends, and there would be time in Rome or Paris. He thought of the tintype he'd taken from a deserter's bag: A woman spanking another woman with the Eiffel Tower in the background. That was rich.

He wondered if Mercy had the breeding and education to present herself properly to the Europeans, if she'd be willing to share him with friends when they traveled, whether she could be trusted to care for things when he went away on business.

O'Rourke's daydreaming had its limits, and after a morning of reveries he was more desperate than ever. When Malkovaich told him that a local politician was coming to inspect the mine the next day, O'Rourke began to plot. McDowell couldn't very well keep him at the mine if the politician offered safe passage elsewhere. Reporters might be present too. His backup plan was simple: to crawl unseen into the trunk of one of the visitors' cars, and once it left the mine he'd be free.

CHAPTER TEN

As Old Man Henderson and his young wife were taking tea in the Sneeds' parlor, his son Jordie, the eldest of several boys from his first wife, who'd died of stomach cancer thirty years earlier, became the first casualty in the industrial war that followed when James O'Rourke, scab clerk, shot him through the neck at a range of 100 yards. It was a spectacular shot, and no one, especially Jordie, could believe it. Only a week before, he'd received two belated medals in the mail from the Canadian government for action in France and Belgium with their engineers. Made it through that war and got it now, here of all places, practically in his own backyard.

"Son of a bitch," he croaked. He lay on the ground squinting into the sun and touched the sunken edges of the hole that went all the way through his neck. Somehow the bullet had missed his windpipe and arteries, and most of his spine. He wasn't even bleeding heavily. He didn't look like he wanted up all that bad, but he struggled a little in confusion. The soles of his boots and the mound of his belly still presented targets for the scab strikebreakers in the mine.

"You killed me, you big dumb son-of-a-bitch," he groaned. "I'm dead."

Bullyrag Greathouse stood in the ditch just off the road where no one else could see him. He held the bolt-action Enfield that belonged to Jordie in his left hand.

"You talk a lot for a dead man," Bully said. "I told you I wouldn't allow it. Not unless we get some declaration of war, and I haven't heard one yet."

Shots were being fired in and out of the mine, sporadically.

"That sounds like a war there, doesn't it?" Jordie asked.

"Didn't have to be that way."

"I could have got my shot off clean if you hadn't interfered. What right do you have? Who the hell's side you on, anyway?"

Bullyrag looked around him. Behind the ditch was a field full of sawgrass and thistle and behind that were woods.

"Jesus, Greathouse. You bastard. You'll pay for this. I could have got that man before he got us."

"Looks like he only got you."

"Fucking Greathouse. Shithouse. Full of yourself and it all stinks."

Jordie Henderson lay in the dirt. He panted and grimaced. Bully watched the road in the direction of the mine and looked around again. He pulled the bolt back and looked to see if a round was chambered.

Jordie said, "Okay, maybe I shouldn't have taken the first shot. But that's all technicalities, Bully. You saw as well as I did that man drawing down on me. You're lucky he didn't hit you too is all."

Bully looked off into the woods.

Jordie gagged but only spit. "Bully, pull me off this road," he said. "I'm a sitting duck. They'll kill me. Help me, Bully."

"I don't know I shouldn't let them do it," Bully said. "Anybody dumb as you should be culled from the breeding stock."

"Very funny. Seriously, help me up. I got to get to the hospital."

Bully stood still. The arms fire around the mine had begun to sound like popcorn. He scratched an itch and looked at Jordie.

Jordie said, "Help me, you bastard, or I'll turn every miner in this country against you. I'll tell them you aided and abetted those pricks in there. Little better than a scab yourself. Your life won't be worth a damn. You should have been the one to get hit. Take my arm and pull me off into the ditch, Bully, please. Come on, get me off this road."

Bully stood looking into the middle distance.

"Your wife is gonna know if you don't, Greathouse."

"What's that mean?"

"It means what it means."

"What's it mean?"

"Force me to tell, and I'll say it means she wears the pants in this strike business, and I don't mean just you but her brother too, what I heard."

"You are one dumb bastard, do you know that?"

101

"Trying to be a man. There's no place for it."

"Always a place for somebody doing the right thing. And I notice you're here today because of her."

"Don't get me wrong, Bully. She's been a great help in all this. Of course she's got to be frustrated."

"What are you saying, Henderson?"

"I don't mean frustrated like that. If anything...."

"Yes?"

"Pull me out of here. Now, Greathouse."

The beginning of something not unpleasant tickled inside Bully. "Maybe you'd like to finish that thought," he said.

"Look, get me out of the line of fire," Jordie said, "and I'll tell you another truth about your wife. Maybe not the sort of truth you particularly want to hear, but the sort a man needs to know anyhow."

Fear and jealousy poured Bully full of rage at those who would presume to control his life.

"You're an asshole, Henderson. But I suppose if I didn't pull you off that road, you and the other men would be pretty upset, wouldn't you?"

"You goddamn right."

"Seeing I got you hurt in the first place."

"Yeah."

"And you'll tell them that."

"That's right, Greathouse. I sure as hell will. Now do it, or you'll be a dead man, you prick."

Bully shot Jordie Henderson in the face. He took the Enfield and walked away at an angle paralleling the long scar of the strip mine. His pants legs snagged on brambles and Queen Anne's Lace, and it was hard going until he came to a field of spiderlike crabgrass. By then he was a quarter-mile north of where he'd left Jordie but still within rifle range of the mine. He saw no one however until he reached another road below the level of the field. The cut slope made a perfect barricade, and union miners were lined up on the berm with rifles jutting over the top like jackstraws.

"Christ, Bully," Dan Hawkins said. "We could have shot you. Get down, will you?"

"Jordie Henderson's dead," Bully said.

Miners gathered around him with interest.

"You were there?"

"I saw the man shoot from inside the mine and hit Jordie twice."

"I heard those shots. I told you they were from inside the mine," a man said.

"But you say they hit him twice?"

Bully nodded. "I tried to get to him, but I couldn't drag him to cover quick enough."

"What were you two doing over there?" Otis Clark asked suspiciously. "That's well inside the ring we've set up. And how did you get his rifle but not get him?"

"Jordie wanted a closer look at the power plant. Said we could blow it with some dynamite if it came to that."

"So they just shot him in cold blood?"

"Yes. And as he fell he threw me his gun."

"He must have known he was done for," Hugh Duncan said. "And he still managed to get you his rifle. A genuine goddamn martyr to the cause."

"Did you see the man shot him?" Clark asked. Clark was a big man too, with the authority of his belly and the righteousness that went with his position in the mine as check weighman, an elective office.

"Yes, I guess I did," Bully said.

"Good. Then you stick close by because when it comes time to pull those scabs out of there I want you to point out the one that started all this."

The men up and down the line repeated his words and nodded in agreement.

A few minutes later, stray bullets thumped into the dirt overhead. Others buzzed overhead, and the strikers pretended to duck but looked over to see.

"Open fire, men," Otis Clark shouted.

The men rose and fired, reloaded and fired again. Some had brought hundreds of rounds neatly packed in boxes, and they shared them around. Others ran out of ammunition quickly for their odd-caliber hunting pieces or ancient hand-me-downs with sights so bent they shot wide anyway. With no weapons to shoot, they tapped the men who still had working guns and begged to take a turn. In that first serious fusillade, hundreds of rounds tore into the mine buildings, boxcars and steam shovels. The

Pinkertons inside returned fire.

The only person to get hit in that first protracted volley was a local miner, Joe Pitkewicius. One of his union brothers on the other side of the mine shot a round in the air with the exhilaration of joining history and the bullet arced over the camp, at its zenith reaching a height of nearly a mile in the pale blue sky, then it fell back down and smashed through the top of Joe's skull like a hammer through a plaster wall.

Five hundred men surrounded the Lester mine by four that afternoon, and their gunfire was a constant roll of thunder. Bully Greathouse sat against the berm, lit a cigarette from the Broad Leaf Tobacco Company of Louisville, Kentucky, and listened to the incredible din of labor versus capital. He felt sorry for Jordie. Dumb bastard tried to manipulate him. Should have made up something he'd believe.

It was hard to think well because of the noise, so Bully sat back and tried to enjoy his smoke but kept coming up with this: If a man thinks something he'll wind up saying it and then you have something to judge him with.

CHAPTER ELEVEN

Earlier that day, Bully had been due home, and Sally was alone with Jordie Henderson, their neighbor at The Crossing. She looked up and said suddenly, "Think of it, Jordie. We're the center. The most radical district in the strongest union in the world. Can't you feel their support radiating like heat?" She looked at him wildly, only partly an act.

Henderson mouthbreathed and looked away. "Is this what the union wants us to do?" he said. "Mr. Sneed's been telling us to be careful, but Mr. Willis and Mr. Hughes made it seem like they wouldn't care if...."

"If what, Jordie?" Sally said.

"If one of us did something to prove how serious we really are about this whole situation. I mean...."

"Jordie. You're talking to me about this because Billy Sneed's my brother. Am I right?"

"Well, that and how you've helped organize the wives. That day your brother spoke out to the Reservoir, you were holding your own meeting. I heard about it. You've done your part, Sally, don't sell yourself short."

"I know I have, but thank you for noticing. If you think that Billy, your president, is hesitant about anything...."

"No, Sally. I wasn't saying that."

"Because we all know the stories of Billy coming under fire twenty years ago in that action at that mine in Carterville."

"I didn't mean anything, Sally."

"Good. We must have unity, as you know full well. And I happen to know that one of the reasons for the tours Billy's been making of the Lester mine is so we could have a good idea of what we're up against. Did you know that? Him scouting for us? Didn't even suspect it was so, did you. So you can see how he's looking at those scabs."

She waited for Jordie to finish the thought, but he stood up. He avoided looking at her and had a peculiar expression, like a boy hesitant to believe.

"He's looking at that mine as a fortification, Jordie. Enemy. I've heard him use the word. And the call may come for us to take that fort."

Her breath could be felt.

"Sometimes, Jordie, we're too limited to see the whole picture because we're caught up in our own little bit. All we see is fish swimming in the lake so we kill and eat them; we lose a child and suffer, we know that; you meet a woman who knows how to love. And so we focus on fish, love and suffering, because it's our piece. But there is a bigger world, and we must try to make it come out the way we'd want it if we thought about it for even half a second. Jordie? If you didn't have to worry for the people you know, or the hardships they'd endure, wouldn't you put in your vote for a more equitable and just world?"

She saw his doubt slacken and thought: usually it's his jaw. She had no idea what form his resolve would take. Not that it mattered. A man like Jordie just needed to be wound up and pointed in the right direction.

Then Bully got home, and she and Jordie talked to him about scouting around the edges of the mine, just to see what was there.

She held Bully tight as he squeezed her up and into him, and she whispered, "Just go with Jordie, baby. I don't think he can do a single thing without your help. I need your strength right now."

"What's he doing here to begin with?" Bully said.

The two men walked together to the crossroads and turned south for the mine. She watched them maternally until they disappeared between the lines of poplars along the road. Funny how they made a pair, Jordie, like a sheaf of dried grass, Bullyrag full of blood and the bull heart to pump it.

She was hanging laundry when Sneed swung by on his way to the embattled mine. Gunshots sounded close enough to be a danger, and Sally calmly hung her underclothes on a rope stretched from a tree to a nail on the house. She looked at Billy with humor.

"Little late for politics, wouldn't you say?"

Sneed grimaced. "What happened out here, Sally?"

"Too late for labor relations? Mediation?"

106

"What's happened?"

"Sounds like a war."

"I'd best not find our men were behind it or there'll be hell to pay."

A walnut fell off a tree onto the tin roof of a neighbor's house, and Sneed ducked at the clang. Sally laughed.

"I don't see what's so funny," he said.

"Billy, when will you learn that justice always prevails?"

"Meaning?" Sneed said. He wasn't listening.

"Remember how you came over here after Ruby was born, all worried her head was squeezed out of shape? You thought nothing would ever go right for her, but it was fine, just as nature intended. Rhythms of the world, Billy. And working men and women everywhere have been put upon for so long that one day we'll not only rise up but also exact our due, and when it's begun there'll be a better life in store."

"You can't believe that, Sally."

She shrugged, took clothespins from a bag and hung her drawers on the line. "Better late than never. Already happened in Russia."

"You've misunderstood entirely," Sneed said. "And your Bolshevik friends have just shown their colors at Genoa. One form of power for another."

"You think you've risen out of our way of understanding things, Billy."

"Things are complicated, Sally. The older I get, the more obvious that is."

"Remember the picture postcards you sent me during the war? I never got to go to any of those lovely places, but even their names were special to me."

"Sally."

"Those romantic lanes, the museums, the groomed gardens with their statues and cafés. All you have to do is trace them back to see it was Indian labor paved the streets, marble sawn from Italian mountains that layered up buildings like cakes, American iron wrought to keep people out. All the good ideas and everyday suffering of everybody who lived upstream of those cities got floated downriver, until finally they clustered someplace like London, where a few certain men got credit for building civilization. But it was us. They belong to us."

"And if everybody claimed their shares, there'd be nothing left at all.

You can't have history in a single generation."

"We might be small but together...."

"You can't think we've been given the right to take lives in the name of some idea so abstract that it doesn't mean anything specific."

Sally laughed, showing lots of teeth. "Like unionism?" she said. "Or would it be patriotism, Billy? Remember the *Maine*!"

Sneed turned for the car he'd borrowed.

Sally laughed some more. "I didn't upset you, did I, Billy?"

"You don't make enough sense to upset me," he said. "Nothing worse than a self-taught thinker."

"Everybody's self-taught," Sally said. "All the great ones."

"Doesn't matter anyway. McDowell and Sheriff Thaxton found Lester finally. He was hiding out in the Great Northern Hotel in Chicago. He's agreed to shut down the mine for the duration. I have to go stop this."

"In the name of what?" she said.

He started the car and put it in gear.

"Democracy? All men created equal?" she called. "Invoke the name of Christ, Billy!" The last she yelled at the retreating car.

She was worried about Bully, though. *Her* man. Her's. Bully hadn't thought it was the best idea. But nobody had been shooting then, so what better time? And the shots now didn't bother her much, since they must be from union men making it hot for the scabs.

A half hour after Sneed left her, Sally saw his car race past, headed west through the crossroads toward Herrin. The gunfire had stopped, mostly. He didn't even look her way so she knew Bully must be fine. She half-filled a pot with water and put it on the stove. Just as it came to a boil she tossed in a handful of coffee grounds. She let the coffee steep and got out her diary. A splash of cold water settled the grounds. She poured carefully from the two-quart pot and blew into the china cup as she stared at the blank pages. Just because Billy hadn't stopped didn't mean Bully was safe. Maybe he'd been hurt but Billy hadn't heard of it. Halfway through her second cup, the gunfire began again in earnest.

Around six, she heard a car pull up and stop near the house. Expecting Bullyrag had gotten a ride and would want his supper, she was surprised to see Fox Hughes instead. He was alone. She thought of him trying something and how she would smash his head in with...there was nothing at hand, which made her madder. She could sense the satisfaction crushing his windpipe would bring. She could do it, too. She squeezed her fingers together until they hurt satisfactorily.

"Sally, I know you'll like this one," Fox said. He swaggered as he came up the yard, and she smelled the stink of his toilet water on the breeze.

She stood under the tin overhang that made her porch and watched him with her shoulder to the post. "What is it you think I'll like, Fox?"

She noted with satisfaction how quickly he changed his demeanor.

"Miss Sally, there's been calls made all over this county looking for the sheriff, the DA, Mr. Sneed, those men that run the chamber of commerce...anybody who would do to slow this thing down. And I've been alone up at union headquarters all day. So they keep calling me, asking did I see so and so, and I could honestly say no, since I ain't seen anybody but Hugh Willis, and that was hours ago. So finally the commander of that National Guard company and the State's Attorney got me on the line and said I had to go out and accept the surrender of them scabs in the mine. Me! I could see there wasn't any way around it but I stayed right where I was until they called to nag me about it again."

"What times are you talking about?"

"The first call came about four. The other was just a few minutes ago. Why?"

"What do you intend to do?"

"Well I sure as hell am not going to be the one to walk fifty scabs out through five hundred miners madder than hornets, especially since they shot some of our boys dead already."

Sally felt as if she were falling. "Who got shot?"

"Jordie Henderson was the first. I don't know. That many shots fired, somebody's going to wind up dead."

"Come on." Sally grabbed Fox Hughes' arm and dragged him away from the house toward the road.

He was laughing. "Damn, Miss Sally. Where you taking me, now?"

They reached the nearest edge of the mine property in minutes. Union men nodded at them in the fading early summer light. Sally couldn't see the men inside the mine, but occasional puffs of smoke came from the buildings, piles of railroad ties and the dirt overburden scraped from the coal vein, and immediately afterward she heard the shots.

She bent over and began pacing the perimeter of their position, asking for Bullyrag, and checking if the men needed anything. Several asked her to tell their wives they were currently engaged, and she said she would. Bully could not be found but had obviously been fine after Jordie's murder by the scabs.

She returned to Fox Hughes, who was standing stupidly in the open, smoking a cigarette and watching as if a troupe of performers was putting on a show for his amusement.

"I don't see any flag of surrender," he told her.

She didn't look.

"No flag of truce whatsoever. What do you think, Miss Sally?"

"I can't find Bully. Help me find him."

"I'm sure he'll turn up, Miss Sally. I got to get back to union headquarters." He grinned. "Somebody's going to call me and ask did I see a white surrender flag, and I have to be able to say, No Sir, I didn't. And that'll be the truth. No white flag anywhere. Just that shot-up white sheet they got hanging off the cookhouse. What do you think, Miss Sally? They just washing their linen?"

He wanted to please her and be recognized for being so bloody clever. She was sick at Bully's absence, sick at the prospect of losing, again, and above all sick of Fox Hughes, the goddamned slick-haired foul-mouthed little turd. She felt like hitting him right in the mouth.

"So what do you think?" Hughes asked, grinning wider all the time.

She thought of what the papers had said about those women in Chicago, the "militant maternalism" Billy had disapproved of. Disapproval, she thought: yet another impediment to life, maybe the most obstinate one. It masked itself as rationality, caution, prudence, benevolence, but was just one more enemy of the good, and the most destructive for all its good manners. She turned to Hughes and said, "You want to know what I think, Fox? Kill 'em. That's what I say. Kill the lot."

Hughes giggled and tossed down his smoke. "Well, now. Damn, Miss Sally. You're quite a woman."

"You wouldn't know what to do with a real woman if you got your hands on one, Fox. Find Bully and tell him I'm looking for him."

"Yes, ma'am. I'll get right on it."

She watched him turn and amble off, and there was some slight satisfaction in setting something else, even him, in motion.

Chapter Twelve

James O'Rourke just happened to have Dean Prochnow's Winchester in his hands when Prochnow asked, "Is that a man down there?" disingenuously, as if he might have placed him there or arranged it.

"Yeah," O'Rourke said. He tried to give the Winchester back to Prochnow, who looked at him and smirked.

"There he is, Ethel," Prochnow said. "You been wondering what the enemy looks like. I'd say he's about five-and-a-half feet tall, skinny but fat in the belly, and has come looking for you with a war rifle in his hands. Thirty-caliber. Nice gun. Rip the head off your neck at this range."

"Here, stop fooling around," O'Rourke said. "There's two of them."

Prochnow peered down through the open gate at the two men facing each other casually on the crown of the road as if they were talking something over. Prochnow grinned.

"Maybe this is it," he said.

"So take your gun. You're the Pinkerton."

Prochnow spit tobacco juice so hard that a little puff of dust rose up to cover it over. "You been dry-firing my rifle until the pin's about wore out," he said. "You're ready to be a Pink too."

"Don't be ridiculous. Here." O'Rourke pushed the rifle's stock against Prochnow's chest. Prochnow made no move to take it. "Would you take this thing?"

"No."

"Take it."

"You wanted to be a man, Ethel. Use it."

"Take your goddamn gun." O'Rourke tried to push the rifle into Prochnow's hands. Prochnow didn't move, O'Rourke let go, and it fell on the ground with a well-oiled clatter.

"Jesus Christ, Prochnow!"

Prochnow could barely hold in his glee. "You should never let your weapon lie around in the dirt, Ethel. You plug up that bore and the barrel's like to blow up in your face."

O'Rourke gasped. "He's going to shoot."

Prochnow looked carefully down at the first man, who did seem to be readying himself. He was turned sideways, squinting their way, but his rifle was still down at his waist. The other man stood by, speaking to him.

O'Rourke tried to run away, but Prochnow grabbed his arm and with a quick twist had O'Rourke's fingers bent against their wrist in some simple but excruciating way that took only one hand to maintain. He pointed down at the Winchester. Its stock was worn dark from Prochnow's cheek.

"Pick up that weapon."

"Prochnow, I can't."

"That man's going to shoot us dead if you don't." Prochnow bent O'Rourke's wrist even more, making him stoop toward the rifle.

"You shoot him," O'Rourke pleaded.

"Nope. Either you do it or looks like we'll die today." He didn't smile, but his eyes narrowed as if he had.

O'Rourke saw the two men arguing, and the one with the rifle yanked back from the bigger man. Again the man raised the gun, and O'Rourke saw the tiny black hole that the bullet would come from.

O'Rourke grabbed the Winchester from the ground, and when Prochnow released him, O'Rourke slapped dirt off it.

"Nope. You do it," Prochnow said when offered the gun. He stood at ease with his hands behind his back and rocked back and forth on his feet.

O'Rourke cocked the lever. A round flew out of the chamber and the next one seated.

"Damn, son. Wasting perfectly good bullets," Prochnow said. He too looked down at the figure of the man looking more likely to shoot. The rifle was up to the man's midriff. "Doesn't matter. We're dead anyway. You're too damn slow, Ethel."

O'Rourke raised the gun with great difficulty, like a ten-foot two-by-four held at one end. He saw that the man intended to shoot. He had no doubt. But then the man lowered the gun, worked the bolt action to chamber a round, and O'Rourke really knew he intended to shoot.

"Prochnow," he begged.

Dean Prochnow looked from the men in the road to O'Rourke and back. "Shoot him, Dickhead!"

O'Rourke put the butt of the stock to his shoulder and pulled it in tight as he'd been taught. He tried to focus on the sights, or the man, but they each came in and out of focus and he felt so dizzy he needed to sit down.

The smaller man with the Enfield squeezed off his shot just as the bigger man grabbed the gun and slap-punched his face. They locked together, holding each other's upper arms, and swung around once as if dancing. The Enfield fell free.

Prochnow grabbed O'Rourke from behind. He put his arms under O'Rourke's armpits and held him upright and in a firing position. Prochnow controlled the rifle now, and he held O'Rourke the way a man might hold a woman from behind to help her make a billiards shot. O'Rourke knew that to the men on the road, it could have looked as if he were alone. But they were still wrestling, and the smaller one was getting the worst of it. Prochnow pulled O'Rourke's limp hand out of the way, slipped his own finger into the trigger guard, sighted past O'Rourke's soft right cheek and fired. The smaller man fell. The big man looked into the mine property at O'Rourke, bent to grab the Enfield and jumped off the road.

Prochnow let O'Rourke go and ducked behind a boxcar, doubled over with laughter. "You did it, Ethel!" he crowed. His face flushed scarlet from laughing at his prank.

Bullets began thumping into the camp, and men dropped what they were doing to take cover behind buildings or stacks of railroad ties or under the boxcars. The Pinkertons standing on the perimeter shot into the woods and the low hills surrounding the mine, but they fired blindly. With no cover they were forced to withdraw to the center of the mine property.

O'Rourke dragged the Winchester under a boxcar with him. He found Tom Meadows, the assistant mine supervisor, there.

Meadows said, "Did you shoot somebody, O'Rourke? What the hell do you have a gun for anyway?" He didn't wait for an answer and low-crawled down the tracks toward the office.

O'Rourke said loudly enough that he hoped Meadows could still hear, "Prochnow, you've killed us all!"

Prochnow giggled, pointing directly into O'Rourke's drained face. "Dumbass," he said.

"*What?*"

"You're going to remember that the rest of your life. That's something you'll be hiding in your lock box 'til the day you die."

"What did you *do* that for?"

"I didn't do it. You did."

Men continued to fire from the camp, and O'Rourke willed himself flat. After more time passed than he could stand, he began to have hope, since skirmishes by definition never lasted long, he was sure he had read it. Yet the guns exploded nearby and popped from afar undiminished.

Then something happened to him, sudden and violent. His air was gone and he was shocked and hurt; only after he began to recover did he understand that the earth herself had kicked him breathless, and it took more time to understand there had been an explosion. He was alive, unhurt, and terrified that there were more things in store that he could not imagine.

"Oh my god jesus christ help me," O'Rourke cried. He lay for a very long time under the boxcar as bullets punctured its steel sides and ricocheted like trapped ball bearings overhead.

"Prochnow," O'Rourke cried.

"Holding that weapon," Prochnow answered. "Being guided by something more powerful and true than you'll ever know again."

When O'Rourke looked at him in fear and confusion, Prochnow busted up laughing. The derision brought O'Rourke back momentarily.

"What are you, shell-shocked?" he said.

"Pain builds character. Remember that."

"Who gave you the right? Whoever told you you could do things like that?"

"These waking dreams," Prochnow said. "Faces out of the past. Places I never been. It's beautiful, Ethel."

O'Rourke shook his head in despair and turned away.

"Here, no, wait, I'm being serious," Prochnow said. "I'll be serious.

Seriously. Listen, forget about those bullets, okay? Really. Forget it. They can't shoot us down here, and they're not going to rush us as long as we've got ammunition. Relax for a minute. Let me tell you the biggest thing in my own life, and then you'll understand why you needed all this to happen. Nothing else has ever come close to its intensity, and that's why I keep it with me all the time and never told anybody until now. Do you want to hear it?

"*Listen to me*," he threatened. "Okay. I was in the Eighty-First Division in France. Right? I told you that."

O'Rourke leaned in, eager for an explanation if only Prochnow would give it quickly.

"We had marched for days, and this on top of fighting for the town of Champillon. Our supply lines hadn't caught up, and the German army had already foraged everything there was to eat. So we were starving, see.

"Wait. I'm not telling it right. You need to help me, like you did with the letter, remember? Tell about whole armies, busted and blown-up, clothes rotting off their bodies, walking wounded and diseased and starving. Staggering around the countryside, and us just a small part of that chaos. My platoon collapsed in some grass next to a road, and it didn't look like we'd be getting up. Done. We were done. Suddenly this flatbed truck coasted down from a grove of trees on a hill, and there wasn't anyone in it but an old farmer, and nothing on the bed but a barrel standing on end, tied down with ropes. The old man pulled up to our position. He could have had a bomb in that thing and set it off before we could have moved, we were so tired. We just watched with our rifles pointed in his general direction. He very slowly got out of the cab, stretched a little like it was another day at work, then climbed up on the back of his truck. He pulled the lid off that hogshead and set it down next to him.

"We didn't know what the hell he had. Could have been *anything*. See? And I bet you can't guess. He reached in and started tossing apples down to us. Imagine it. Apples as scarlet-red as cocks' combs and shined up like every person in his village had taken turns rubbing them on their shirts. My god: apples falling like stars from the rough hands of a filthy Frog farmer on the back of a Ford in the middle of that war. I'll *never* forget that."

O'Rourke stared, waiting, but Prochnow seemed to have left him to

115

live in that other moment. "So what are you telling me?" he interrupted jealously.

"I'm not telling you anything. I'm showing you."

"Showing me what?"

"The most important thing in the world, Ethel." Prochnow smiled dreamily.

"What, that an army marches on its stomach?"

"Nope."

"That the apple was a sign that the worst was over and you were going to make it?"

"Don't be stupid. Half of us were killed a few days later at Epernay when German sappers caught us sleeping."

"So are the apples Garden of Eden apples? You know, fighting your way to them was the price you paid for the knowledge?"

"Nope. Just apple apples. Really shiny ones. A little tart, as I remember."

"What's it *mean*, you simp?" O'Rourke cried. "I can't stand it how everybody's always got all the answers but none of it ever makes any sense. I try so hard, but I never understand *anything*."

Prochnow smiled and blotted his eyes nostalgically.

The union men blew a small earthwork dam that held back water for the mine, hoping to flood the entire property and drive out the scabs, but the retention pond was too far away to do any good. When they could, they rushed in to try to set fire to rail cars, blow up steam shovels, and take over areas of the camp, but each time the mine guards drove them a short ways out and the slow exchange of fire began again. This went on until the light failed and the shooting slowed, and when it was very late, men tried to sleep in shifts. Prochnow told O'Rourke what to do.

"Sit here, Ethel," he said in a kind, tired voice. "Sit on the edge of this box. Further over. More. More. There. If you fall asleep, you'll fall off the damn thing and wake up. Okay? If anything moves, shoot it. Remember: you're a killer now, so you might as well do what you can to save your own life. I have to sleep."

"I can't, Prochnow," O'Rourke said. "I can't stay awake, I never shot anybody, I can't do anything. You have to help me."

"Do something on your own for once, Ethel. Save your own skin, or do some goddamn thing. I got something kicking in here and I need to dope off for a little while, and I mean right now."

"Nobody in the world acts like you," O'Rourke whined. "When we get out of here, I'm telling everybody about you. You're deranged. I'm not to blame for this."

Prochnow paused, seeming to consider seriously. "The doctors said if I can function that it means I'm not shell-shocked, just a little run-down."

He pulled a big evil dagger from his right boot and put the tip under O'Rourke's nose. There was still more amusement than malice in his tired eyes.

"A war eats everything, like some monster brat. But life goes on anyway, so whatever it ate up wasn't worth much to begin with. Not in any sense that matters. We're free, O'Rourke. Do what the hell you want. If we survive this thing, I'm going to put everything I've got into what little holds its value. Like those apples I mentioned. From now on."

He tilted the blade up, just a little, so the tip went into the cartilage of O'Rourke's nose.

"Damn, Prochnow, you stuck me!" O'Rourke cried and wiped away blood.

"Well, I pulled it right back out again," Prochnow said. He waved the knife goodbye and padded off toward the cookhouse.

Sporadic gunfire continued around the camp, but none of the other men seemed worried anymore, just exhausted, as if the noises had little to do with their situation. Prochnow lay on his back behind a wall of cordwood near the cookhouse, his boots sticking out ridiculously. O'Rourke gripped the Winchester and tried to convince himself not to sleep. To sleep meant death, or capture and its terrors. He began to cock the lever of the rifle, thought better of it, and got the web of skin between his thumb and forefinger caught in the action. He nearly screamed but was embarrassed, and the pain kept him going a while.

He started dozing and jerking awake and silently thanked Prochnow for his trick with the crate. It saved him a few times, but he became more and more skillful at balancing and fell more deeply asleep each time. Suddenly he woke, terrified, to find that more than an hour had passed in which he had been completely unconscious and might have been killed. What if he *had* been killed and was dead? Surely the afterlife wasn't just a continuation of the same misery. But how could one know? Maybe

117

Prochnow was the ghost of somebody killed by the Germans. He felt rested now anyway and tried to think of something pleasurable to keep himself alert and amused.

There was Oak Street Beach in the blazing city summers, the vendors with bottles of syrups to pour on the balls of shaved ice, people bathing in the Lake, entire neighborhoods of families sleeping on sidewalks or in the parks because of the heat. Concerts in the band shell, sailboats rocking gently at anchor. The amusements of White City or the fortunetellers' booths on the end of Navy Pier, where the Grand Ballroom hosted the likes of Colonel Roosevelt and the Gettys. He would drive with Mercy up Half-Day Road through Millionaire's Row and point out the castle towers of Northwestern University, saying, "That's where I received my education." Mercy or a girl like her but with different hair and something in her eyes turned and said in a hostile voice, "Why don't you get off it, you silly clot?"

He woke grumpy, tired and frighteningly cold. It was still dark. His body knew it was hurt somewhere, and when he stirred his calves ached and his neck and back proved stiff beyond belief. He hoped his back wouldn't go out now, of all times, and leave him helpless; he might need to fight his way out of here. He could do that, he assured himself. He'd be good at it.

It was quiet now, his ears rang with it, and he was sure the worst was over. Daydreaming was boring too, he decided. Prochnow and his visions. He felt cheated. Trying to imagine something better now was as futile as trying to enjoy a bottle of wine and a good dinner when you were hungover as hell. He felt he'd rather be dead than to feel as awful as he did. He put the rifle next to him where he could easily reach it in case, stretched mightily and lay down to get a proper sleep.

CHAPTER THIRTEEN

Sneed paced the parlor. He held his glasses in his hand and sweated coldly. He had never noticed how little free floor space there was in their house. He couldn't walk, there were so many *things* in the way, and, pacing, he tried to name them as if it were the First Day: wingback, footstool, plant stand, radiator, settee, divan, butler's table, upright piano, bookcases with dentils under crown molding. The junk of materialism when what was needed....

"Please," Cora said. "Look at yourself. Stop. Stop."

Sneed faced the small woman who blocked his path. Her face irritated him with yet another demand, but it was soothing to be told to stop, and he wanted her to refute him entirely.

He sat. "What have I done, Cora? Even now I feel if I can respond to this thing properly it'll go away."

"No one can change it now." Cora put her hand on the back of his neck.

Her palm was cool, and he put it on his forehead. It made him feel feverish. He leaned forward to stand, but she pressed him back into the chair.

"Lester's men took jobs they knew to be tantamount to strikebreaking, and the union men are playing their fool parts. It'll end when both sides have had their say. That's all."

"How could you understand?"

Cora's eyes widened. "I understand," she said, growing quieter, "because I have shared every part of your life for twenty-one years. I've kept this home so that if any of your cronies or constituents dropped by at any hour of the day or night it would not shame us. I've raised our children while you were on the road. I watched this community suffer and heard what they said about me even as I fed them. I see how you work and study and finish what you start, and how these people respect you and in some cases worship you. I know exactly what you've done all week, and where you've done it, and you didn't have to tell me a thing. Not that you ever do."

"So you tell me what I've done," he said, falling back into the chair and resting his head against its leather wing.

"You have done your job. And before you say that's too simple, think about it. You've spoken your mind in good faith with your usual concern for those in your charge. You've been seen, given support, and tried to please John Lewis, Egypt, and Springfield all at once. I think you've done very well indeed. As usual."

Sneed looked up. He felt a tiny hope. "Do you think so?"

"Of course. Will, you think all the way around to the back side of truth sometimes, simply because you can and then you get confused. Eat something now? It's nearly midnight."

"Eat? I need to work."

"Work at what?"

He sagged again. "I don't know."

"I think you should leave for Springfield, Will," Cora said quietly. She avoided his gaze. "Tonight. Now, after supper."

"My god! You *do* think I'm to blame."

"No. Men like that brute Jansen are to blame, and so is Lester, dictating from afar."

"Then what are you saying?"

"It'll be better for you."

"For me? You've been making demands on me in the name of the family all along. Why change your tune now? What about the other families?"

Cora knelt next to him and massaged his shoulder with one hand. Her fingers dug into the muscles and tendons. It felt good. It hurt a little. She's strong, he realized.

"It's best for all of us," she said. "You must distance yourself from whatever happens. If it comes to murder, your career will end, and you might even be indicted. If it doesn't then no harm done. But you must keep perspective. The senate is more important than the union..."

"Now wait..."

"You have to go up for the Constitutional Convention in a few days anyway. And above all you must be sure to save your credibility as senator. Without it, everyone will suffer, including the union. You've thought I was being selfish, Will, I know, but it wasn't selfishness. Yes, I want our family to live well, free from hardship, but I'd go back to that little house on Seventeenth Street before I'd see you shamed or have this community's name blackened. We all need you. Go to Springfield. Now."

Sneed's mind roiled with possibilities and their possible outcomes. He couldn't seem to think at all. Cora got up and fixed a late supper. He ate it and tried to think. She left him alone and puttered domestically as if it was midday, not midnight.

A good woman, he thought. I would be a ruin if she were not here. Better off. But she's right: If this, then that. More time passed.

If the Socialists ever regained their power, this event would be moot, just another heroic step along the path, and claiming one's part in it advantageous. If capital got the upper hand, they'd portray Herrin in the media as the lunatic fringe, and labor would blame Herrin for dashing the hopes of working people forever. Maybe not forever, since everything went in cycles, but it might set the cause back a hundred years.

He determined to act decisively and tried several unsuccessful calls. To show himself now at Lester's mine would not only make him complicit, he would run the risk of public humiliation if his men refused him or laughed at his naïve demand they stand down. In many ways, he didn't blame them, and if a couple of things had been different in his own situation, he might.... He could sense, at a safe distance, the satisfactions of the mob, but he would never admit that to Cora or anyone else.

Sneed looked in on his children and held Cora tightly before going across the street and waking Van Buren to offer him money to borrow his car. Van Buren refused payment and said it was his honor and duty.

Sneed began to drive after two in the morning. He felt sure he could stay awake, and Cora had put hot coffee in a Thermos bottle. He drove south along Park Avenue when he should have gone north toward the state capital. Park Avenue narrowed; the homes receded into the countryside away from the road. His heart thumped a bloody rhythm on his eardrums. Still two miles from the Lester mine, he could see the glow of fire and feel the bass stutter of a machine gun. He wheeled Van

Buren's car back to the north, passed his own home, now dark, and drove through downtown Herrin. He paused at the turnoff for Route 2. If he went left, he went to Colp. Right, to the highway for Springfield. He took the right road. He hoped it was the right road.

It was confusing to think that just when you discovered you were good at something—politics, oratory—it might be necessary to use your will *not* to practice it, even when the skill seemed benign.

What he'd meant was simple: *There is a fight on....* But fight meant violence.

In the struggle for.... One thing fighting for survival with another and back to violence.

If we join together.... There. That was in fact what he had said. *We must join together in order to resist-repulse-repel....* More exclusion and violence.

If there was no way to express the concepts, he wasn't to blame. Words betrayed because they refused to speak truth. No, he loved language too much to believe that. Truth was, words betrayed those who couldn't handle their power. They betrayed pretension, falsehood, confused thinking.

After all Egypt *was* in a fight for its life against forces that would never relent unless confronted with sufficient strength, and there was no way of softening that. On the other hand, there was public opinion, a separate thing, and surely the way of the future.

Chapter Fourteen

At dawn Prochnow didn't bother to wake him or be angry. He was withdrawn and apathetic. The rest of the frightened scabs looked outward to the silent fields and shivered, soaked with dew. McDowell told Malkovaich and another man to go back to the cookhouse and find some breakfast for everybody. The two rummaged and came back with what they said was the best they could do under the circumstances, doling out to each man a handful of dried macaroni and some salt. The men crunched it in their jaws like bones and passed around a tin can of greasy cold coffee with grounds floating on top like river debris. Another hour passed.

"Halloo, the mine!" a man called from the woods.

"What do you want with us?" McDowell yelled.

Other union men began to call from their positions. O'Rourke thought they sounded tired and mollified, as if they'd gotten their feelings out through that long night and were now in brotherhood with the out-of-towners they'd terrorized. They yelled for the scabs to leave their guns behind, come on out and be escorted out of the county in safety. The men in the camp began to discuss it. Some feared a trick but wanted to be done with this, and some were angry at the idea of surrender. They fought among themselves.

"Come on out!" the union men hollered from the fields and woods. "We're peaceful!"

"It's okay, come out of there! We ain't gonna hurt ye!"

Inside the camp there was more confused talk of dwindling ammunition, food, and water, and of what demands could be made to ensure their safety, until impatiently one man and then two more began to grab their bags and loose belongings in preparation for surrender, and the others followed suit. Mine guards burned their employment papers and tossed their guns into the pit or the weeds.

The instant the scabs went forward with hands on their heads, yelling they gave up, there was wild shooting in the air and men began running toward them. When the two groups met, a little man on the union side ordered everyone to stop firing. Waving a large pistol loosely as if it were too heavy for his grip, he declared, "I am leader of this bunch."

Several of the others told him to shut up or they'd shoot him and all the prisoners too, and they began punching scabs with fists and swinging rifle butts to prove their point. The peacemaker strode forward to grab a rifle from one of his brother's hands, but three other men stopped him, took his gun, and held him by the back of his neck like a little dog and forced him to watch.

A new leader emerged, fifty, fat, rawfaced. He used the same tactics as the little man, but this time the union men listened.

"First order of business," he said. "Clark, come here. You say Greathouse knows about this? Get Greathouse up here. Greathouse. Bully, get up here. Point out the sumbitch that shot Jordie Henderson and started all this."

O'Rourke recognized Bully Greathouse as the man wrestling Prochnow's victim, and he thought again, his shanks itching terribly in the heat, how it might have looked like he shot this man's friend dead.

Bully Greathouse scanned the crowd slowly, surely, with the theatrics of heavy consideration. Under his gaze each of the scabs looked down or away, hoping they wouldn't be the one identified, even though they were pretty sure they hadn't fired the *very* first shot. Greathouse's eyes looked into O'Rourke's, passed him up, came back, and moved on again. O'Rourke thought he might pass out. With near-hysterical relief he heard Greathouse say, "Him," and everyone looked up to see him pointing at McDowell, the mine manager. Otis Clark nodded once at the mob's leader, who gave orders to march these murderous outlaws away from their illegal concern.

The prisoners were formed into one long column, marched a hundred yards down the road and halted. O'Rourke heard a man at the front say clearly, "No belongings. You take nothing with you. Empty all your pockets and bags."

The order was passed down the line, each union man repeating some version of it, until it reached the old man guarding O'Rourke. The old-timer turned to O'Rourke and said, "What did they say? Can you tell me what they said?"

"They said we're to empty our bags and pockets," O'Rourke said.

The old man nodded gratefully and motioned for O'Rourke to comply.

Another union man listening nearby interrupted them. "Shut the hell up and do what he says. You won't need anything where you're going."

O'Rourke lay the contents of his pockets neatly on the dirt in front of his toes. Quarter, nickel, two pennies. Keys to the commissary files and cabinets on a metal ring. A celluloid comb. His pen, from one breast pocket, and a letter to Mercy from another. He stood for a long while as union men stormed up and down the line and yelled for everyone to work faster. One of them thought the scabs should take off their shoes and socks, and when its imaginative value was realized, the order repeated itself up and down the line. O'Rourke's folded paychecks fell from his right sock and fluttered just out of reach. He stepped out of line to retrieve them but a miner moved in and slapped the back of O'Rourke's head so hard that he winced and shook his own fingers.

"You didn't empty your bag!" he yelled. His spit landed on O'Rourke's face. "Empty it," he said. "Empty everything." He raised his pistol dramatically to O'Rourke's temple and widened his eyes.

O'Rourke hurriedly dumped the valise of his belongings and collected geegaws. A tin of soap powder, a straight razor, hairbrushes, silver belt buckles, a pocket watch, the pornographic print. The bully with the pistol wasn't satisfied nor were his fellows. They shouted contradictory commands until they were hoarse, over cries of pain drifting up and down the line. O'Rourke's tormentor kicked at his things, uninterested in the contents of the bag but aware he wasn't doing as much as the others.

"I thought I told you to empty everything," he said, looking up the line.

"I did, sir. I did, you can see, there's nothing left. Look." O'Rourke pulled his trouser pockets inside-out, picked the lint off the tips and set it free in the breeze.

"I told you to empty *everything*," the man said. He picked up the box of soap and threw it on O'Rourke's feet. "So empty it."

O'Rourke opened the box and poured the soap powder out on the ground.

Other miners pointed and laughed. "What in hell are you doing?" someone said. "Look, hey Tim, look, we tell them to empty everything, and shit-for-brains empties his soap box. What'd you do that for? You got a gun hidden in there?"

The scabs were ordered to lie face down on the ground. It was still early and the dew stuck the dirt to O'Rourke's lips and eyelashes. The mob leader seemed to be redressing his men. Another five minutes passed in near silence while someone looked for line to bind the captives' hands. When a man brought a coil of it back at a run, it was cut into two-foot lengths and distributed so each cluster of miners could truss its scab. In the end the lengths ran out, and O'Rourke, lying near the end of the column, was told to keep his wrists together at the small of his back and pretend he was tied.

O'Rourke was determined to make a good impression on his captors and held his arms behind him vigorously. It made it hard to breathe. He watched his paychecks blow down the line, and the pornographic Paris photo was ground into the dirt by a boot. Other scabs' belongings blew past. A letter typed on a sheet of onionskin paused near his face long enough for him to read, "Why in the hell don't you send the money for the rent. I am in need." It was signed, "Your wife, Pearl Davis." It was written like a business letter, and the return address in the upper left corner was in the 4600 block of Prairie Avenue, Chicago. O'Rourke didn't know the neighborhood.

The scabs were ordered to their feet and again marched single-file up the road toward Herrin, the mob pistol-whipping them as they shuffled along, pushing them to the ground and then dragging them up and yelling that they were out of line. There was a lot of laughter. O'Rourke sweated at the thought of being struck, and he knew that someone could die accidentally in the slow five miles to Herrin.

They had walked only a half-mile when they were ordered to stop again at a crossing. A dozen ramshackle shacks stood in the northeast corner. Women, several holding babies, came running from their homes.

Now the mob took on a different tone. The big man, Bullyrag, yelled at the women to go home. One of them ran to him, and he pulled her to the side to talk. The voices of the miners rose, and there were feminine rages among them now. Greathouse and the woman who appeared to be his wife argued fiercely.

The old man guarding O'Rourke said with surprise and delight, "That's Bullyrag and Sally. The other's Otis Clark. He's from Number Nine. That's where I worked. I worked there twenty-two years. My boy's started as an electrician there now. There's a real trade in that."

Clark stepped over to the couple and said something. Bullyrag shook his head. The woman looked at her husband defiantly then followed Clark down the line. Clark was about thirty-five, had a strong nose and jaw, and wore a fedora with his overalls. Sally was a big woman, O'Rourke thought, matched to her big husband. She held her child as if it was an integral part of her; the little appendage bounced with her jog and looked at the scene as neutrally as a god.

Clark and Sally stopped before they reached O'Rourke. They pulled the mine superintendent out of the line with the help of several of their men eager to do the right thing.

McDowell said, "Boys, I can't keep up. I got a wooden leg. Please, let me rest. I can't keep up."

Bullyrag stepped forward, and there was another argument. Sally was against him. Otis Clark took McDowell by the arm and motioned for his attendants to follow. Bullyrag and his wife came along too, still arguing. Clark dragged McDowell fifty feet down the road. An underling hit him over his left eyebrow with a pistol butt. McDowell fell. Clark shot him in the stomach, and McDowell drew up reflexively. Sally had a pistol in her hand and tried to make Bullyrag take it. He refused by ignoring her.

O'Rourke heard her yell, "What sort of man is not for his family!"

Clark shot McDowell again, in the chest. Bullyrag turned and began to walk away from them. His wife screeched Bully! Bullyrag! Oscar! He didn't turn around. Another man fired a bullet into McDowell's forehead. Clark, the other men, and Sally with her baby rejoined the procession.

The prisoners were marched forward again. Otis Clark was now in charge due to his decisive actions at the Crossroad. He maintained order as the first leader had, by shoving and threatening both scabs and his own men. They had gone only a hundred yards when a large black auto pulled up and forced the line of prisoners and their captors to the side of the road. O'Rourke noticed a star on the grill. He didn't know what that meant, but the rear plate said "Congressional" in small stamped letters above the plate number. O'Rourke nearly cried with relief. It was the politician who had toured the mine, and anyone in the government would put an immediate end to the brutality.

"That's the President," the old man walking with O'Rourke said.

"No, it's the senator," O'Rourke said.

"What did you say?"

It didn't seem to matter. The driver who stepped from the car was not Sneed's driver, and the man he opened the back door for was not the senator. Mutters of "State Board" rippled in both directions from the car, which was parked near the center of the line.

Hugh Willis put his hands on his hips and in a low voice questioned Clark. Willis' face was angry. He gestured to his right at the scabs in the front of the file, then to the left at the scabs in the rear. Otis Clark stood and listened. When he replied he was calm, holding the stock of his rifle in his armpit, the barrel drooping down, pointed at Willis' feet. Sally Greathouse charged them furiously, and Willis stepped back. The woman raged, O'Rourke could hear her plainly, but she seemed to be speaking in tongues. It was impossible to imagine that any of it—rage, guns, men with authority over life or death—had anything to do with him.

Willis appeared to be considering. He stared off into the distance with his chin lifted, eyes steady, and for short seconds there were no engines, no shouts, no feet on the march, no gunfire or groans. Nothing consequential of man at all, and O'Rourke saw for the first time the details of the Southern Illinois he'd been reporting to Mercy. The sun stood a hand's width above the tree line. It had already changed from blood-red to midmorning yellow. Later it would be a white-hot disc. The maples and oaks shook their leaves in a dusty green field rippling under gusts of wind, and the blue skies were cloudless and impossibly deep, as in a dream. Somewhere, someday, he wouldn't be afraid of things. They'd be the same things as here, of course, but he'd understand and they would save him in the end. He would be a better man. A man.

Hugh Willis inhaled sharply and said, "Listen, don't go killing these fellows on a public highway. There are too many women and children around to do that. Take them over in the woods and give it to them. Kill all you can. Kill them all." He and his driver returned to their car and clipped a couple of their own men with the front bumper as they left.

A cheer came from the union sympathizers at the front of the line. It took several minutes due to inefficiency and too much excited talk—*Hot damn a turkey shoot; Try out this new shotgun; Is this right?; What do I get if; Get going; Stop; Line up*—but the scabs were finally facing a tree line twenty feet away. Far through the dark woods another field showed brightly between the trunks. The miners that had guns stood behind the scabs. Those without regretted it deeply, and vowing never to get caught without again, and agreeing with each other that preparedness was a simple virtue, they stood on the road like an eager audience to a potato-sack race.

O'Rourke heard Otis Clark say, "Here's where you run the gauntlet, bastards. See how fast you can run to Chicago, damn you!"

A shot was fired. O'Rourke stood there stupidly, dazed, wondering how it had come to this as men on both sides sprinted for the tree line. The only other man who did not run lay in the weeds with gray matter bulging from his forehead.

O'Rourke began to run as if in a nightmare, heavily, losing his feet and pitching forward. The crash of gunfire came from everywhere, all at once, and he wasn't sure he wasn't running straight into it. Just inside the trees a line of heavy posts was strung with four strands of barbed wire that began at shin-level and came up to the chest. Men fell on the wire and screamed as it ripped their skin. Like rats they piled on one another against the wire, jumped over each other, pushed each other down. Some began slipping between the strands or falling flat and crawling under them. The strikers advanced and shot into them. Only the necessity of reloading and the mechanical limits of their weapons kept them from firing more.

O'Rourke felt a blow to his right calf and immediately another on his left buttock. He ran up to the fence, stopped, backed away a few steps, vaulted it and collapsed on the other side. He lay in heavy undergrowth and felt something hot soaking his trousers, which he was afraid to touch. He crawled instinctively to a honeysuckle bush and fell back into it, the canes poking him and jabbing at his eyes, but he squirmed and smashed them with his back until the outside world was hidden, and, he hoped, he was hidden from the killers. The canes bent into a sort of wicker chair, and live vines covered over his entry. He felt pride at his instincts despite his city breeding. It was dusty inside the den, and he tried to stop gasping for air but that only made his heart pound so hard and fast he wondered if it would hold up.

If O'Rourke moved his head just so, he could see a little of what was happening, but most of it was like something heard on a radio in the next room, disembodied and terrible. Those caught on the far side of the fence were being tortured and shot at point-blank range. One man was beaten with gun stocks so solidly that O'Rourke heard the thuds against his bone even over the man's screams for help. Above the din, a miner shouted, "You big son-of-a-bitch, I *can* kill you." A shot, and the screaming stopped.

A man yelled, "Shoemaker!" By the sound of it, several miners had gathered in admiration over the assistant superintendent's capture. They shot him and shot him three more times after that.

O'Rourke thought he heard Prochnow roaring in anger but realized he wouldn't know what Prochnow would sound like angry—he'd never spoken other than conversationally—and he wondered whether Prochnow would turn into a berserker or accept his fate passively. He hoped for Prochnow's sake he would...what? He didn't know what to hope for.

After twenty minutes shots could still be heard at a distance in different quarters, but O'Rourke heard nothing nearby, no footsteps, voices, whimpers of pain. He leaned forward from his seat in the honeysuckle copse, and the canes snapped loudly under his shifting weight. His legs had fallen asleep, and the pain from their awakening far exceeded the dull ache of his wounds. He froze to see if the bush betrayed him but nothing seemed to hear or even to care that he'd survived.

He crawled on hands and knees in the high grass along the fence. Mutilated corpses sat and lay all around and were horrible to see. Shreds of flesh and hair stuck to the barbs on the wire.

Prochnow hung from an enormous solitary oak. His face was swollen black and the thick purple tongue stuck out between his lips in derision. O'Rourke sobbed and crawled until his knees could no longer bear his weight, then he stood, walked, ran. He ran from the woods, across a road, through a field of hummock grass that threw him off-balance, and he felt the intense pleasure of flight. In the near distance he spotted a farmhouse with a root cellar with an outside entrance. Like a rabbit straight for the warren, O'Rourke instinctively made for the hole under the house. He struggled with the heavy doors, lifted one up to his chin, threw it back with an iron clang, and dove into the cool spidery cellar. No sooner had he stretched full-length, face-down, on the earthen floor than he heard the car and the whoops of the men in it.

"Back that way. Edge around. Around, around. Go go go go go go go." The man yelled to make himself heard over the motor, and O'Rourke knew he thought he was being stealthy.

The five of them had no fear and dragged him from the cellar by his feet so rapidly the stone steps banged his ribs. There wasn't much room in the Model T, and they discussed strapping him across the hood like a deer. Finally they threw him in the back seat, where one of the men sat on him; two others rode on the running boards all the way to Herrin. A hole had rusted through the floor pan, and O'Rourke watched, carsick, as the world sped past under his face, only a foot away, dangerous and dizzying, dirt, grass, blacktop, gravel, more dirt. The actors in the meaningless pageant whooped and hollered with glee over their victory until, as they entered the outskirts of town, their commotion attracted other cars, and the procession achieved the air of a parade.

O'Rourke heard the cars full of men cheering and singing. Someone yelled there were others at Southside, and the car turned sharply and raced along at full speed for several minutes.

The men pulled O'Rourke from the car and threw him to the ground next to several other captives. They were in an elementary school playground, and spectators sat in the swings, bending and straightening their legs, rocking themselves gently as they watched. Others lined the teeter-totters and the small merry-go-round. Even more stood or paced hungrily, ready for whatever was to come. Eventually hundreds of men, women, and children had gathered.

O'Rourke didn't recognize Malkovaich's swollen, bloody face until a man in the mob yanked open Malkovaich's army shirt, popping the buttons off it.

"Take that off, you cowardly son-of-a-bitch," he said. "You never served in no army."

"I did, sir."

"Did's ass. Get it off. You make me sick."

"Damn, Tom, look at this." Another man had been searching the captives' clothes. "He wasn't lying. Old boy got around." He waved discharge papers. "Private Antonio Malkovaich, Headquarters Company,

305th Signal Corps, 80th Division. Action at Somme, St. Mihiel and Meuse-Argonne."

Tom kicked Malkovaich in the ribs. "Polack. Cunt. You think the Somme was something? You wait."

The crowd taunted and spit on the six bleeding men until a consensus was reached that they should be forced to crawl down Stotlar Street to the cemetery a mile away as a symbol of something. They had crawled just fifty feet when the mob got impatient and told them to walk. Young boys raced around the edges of the crowd and competed to find bigger and bigger pebbles to throw, until someone had to tell them to stop because it was pitiful to watch boys get that excited and struggle with rocks they couldn't even pick up. It took forty minutes to cover that mile in the humidity and heat, and the wounds of the six bled openly.

The exhausted prisoners finally stood shaking on the north side of the cemetery. Sycamores stood in a row along the road with trunks whitewashed with lime as high as a man could reach. The plots were filled with Herrins, Stotlars, and other founding names, and an American flag waved by the arched entrance. It was a beautiful place, a republic of stones.

Someone called for Jeremy Brown to bring that goddamned rope. Jeremy pushed through the crowd, wearing a navy summer wool jacket and holding a bight of line. He stretched out the hemp, made a small loop in each hand and slipped the clove hitch over the first man's head. He pulled it tight until the man's eyes bugged and he gagged. Jeremy paid out a few feet of line and did the same to the second man, until all six were yoked together by their necks. He worked quickly but made sure the spacing between men was equal and went back to adjust a knot or two just to be sure it was all done right.

A man with a gun hugged Jeremy across the shoulders with one arm and said, "See, boy? We like you better than we do them. You're more like one of us than they are, and they're white men."

The mob believed the sheriff was coming, and there was movement and noise.

"If you've never prayed before you'd better do it now," a woman said.

"'Nearer my God to Thee,'" the man next to her quoted and laughed.

She sang back gorgeously, "When e'er a cloud appears in the blue /

132

Remember somewhere the sun is shining / And so the right thing to do is make it shine for you."

The couple kissed.

The first shot hit O'Rourke in the heel, and when he fell he dragged the others to the ground by their necks. Several people shot the men on the ground with pistols. It looked like they might all be dead, but one of the mob shot each one again for good measure. Luckily, there were only six scabs, and his revolver was fully loaded.

The mob watched some of them still struggling.

Jeremy Brown unfolded a clasp knife he kept in his right back pocket in place of a wallet. He moved forward; the crowd breathed and were eyes. Jeremy knelt next to each body lying in the grass in the graveyard and slit the throats. The knife was dull.

Some time later O'Rourke came to. He was having trouble breathing and his body ached with thirst, a need identical to that for air. He begged and someone began to come to him from very far away with a toy pail of water. The approach took a long time, much too long, and the mob intervened to make the water bearer pour it uselessly on a grave.

O'Rourke shivered, both burning and freezing in agony. A woman stepped in front of the sun and shielded his eyes from the glare. She stood against the entire sky, her head haloed by pure energy, an infant on her hip looking down with double chins and graven jowls. She turned to speak and her face was a silhouette cut by artists on the Lakefront. The woman had saved him from the sun's brilliant torture, and O'Rourke's tears of gratitude were so intense, personal, and genuine that he knew *this* was love: being helpless and having another still care. He slipped away and, no longer aware of his impending death, felt himself sitting humbly and contentedly with someone, watching the parade go past, exhausted but glad to be alive. A glowing Christ pumped the brakes on his little truck and Gabriel tossed down candy to the people on the curbs.

"Mercy," O'Rourke choked out through blood and spit.

"He wants mercy, Sally. Give him just a taste."

The brilliant mother put her booted foot on O'Rourke's chest.

"I'll see you in hell before you hurt my baby anymore with your scabbing," she said and leaned into it hard.

With the added pressure, O'Rourke's blood welled from his wounds like hot springs from deep in a rock.

"Oh," O'Rourke cried.

"Some people would bitch if they was being hung with a new rope," a man in the crowd said.

We all laughed.

"Not a bad idea. Let's jerk him to Jesus!"

We deeply regretted there wasn't time for a lynching, but one of us was able to take a long hot piss on the bodies, drawing circles, aiming playfully at upturned faces, before the law arrived and we dissipated like fog.

No one will believe us, but we really did grieve in our hearts at the actions of those corrupt sadistic few. We've tried so hard in our many voices to love each other over the years but living in Babel is no mean feat. We're not mean, you understand, just enthusiastic. Free will is a sickness in the soul.

Listen: You won't like this much, but by reading this far you never stopped any of this either, so you're one of us now. And for that reason alone we deserve some small sympathy and understanding.

CHAPTER FIFTEEN

Dawn came, and Sneed was still sitting up against down pillows. He knew he needed to be fit to face the inquisitors, but sleep was impossible and waking an uncanny nightmare. He knew he should rise, bathe and dress. An hour later he still stared at the same piece of wall. He wondered if this was a breakdown. It would be true only if he didn't get up.

Get up. If you do it now. Now. And now. Come on, you can do it. Get up, Bill. Let's go. I can do this, just start by getting off the bed.

He noted the shift in pronouns and wondered how many were involved in the negotiation. He forced himself up. It frightened him that his toilet and breakfast were so completely inconsequential, like everything else. Before he could go the phone rang.

When he hung up there was a new use for the energy seething in him. Senator McCall, of all people, that jerk, just a mouthpiece for chambers of commerce and industry. All of them with their dirty little secrets, their money, deceptions. *They* helped bring this on, and now they would try to use it to discredit working people everywhere by making Egypt an example. As he finished dressing he began to compose in his mind:

Is he less to blame who lit the match that finally caused the explosion of human passions, and all for the hope of gain? Their thievery of our resources is all the more pernicious for being sanctioned, taxed and organized by this state....

Chapter Sixteen

When Cora Sneed went to visit the wounded in Dr. Black's hospital the afternoon after the attack, she found one of the victims propped up with pillows in a bed on the second floor. There were flowers in the corners of the room, on the windowsill, on his bedside tray, and he was surrounded by newsmen from cities across the United States. She saw several miners and other Herrin residents standing in the back of the ward. Other wounded men lay still on their beds and listened. A reporter for the Brooklyn *Evening American* sat on the edge of the bed and wrote as the injured man spoke.

"I'll start again from the beginning, gentlemen, for those of you who just arrived," he said. He adjusted his throat bandages as if the gauze were a cravat. "You'll have to forgive my hoarseness. I think I may be coming down with something."

The crowd laughed.

"My name is Patrick O'Rourke, and I was a guard at the mine. I've been a lot of things in my day—soldier, cowboy, track-layer, speculator. I've made and lost a dozen fortunes, and I guess you could say I've started over each time just for the fun of it. But sometimes the wisest course is to admit your defeat, and I'm not one to hide from that fact. The people of Williamson County have bested all of us at the Lester Mine, and I take my hat off to such worthy opponents."

The miners and other townies grinned and nodded their appreciation, and some of the newsmen looked at them amusedly or with a touch of admiration or jealousy.

"And really we must understand we are brothers and sisters in the same pursuit: the bettering of the American way of life. We just came at the opportunity differently, am I right?"

The crowd in the ward murmured it was so.

"We are the same body, but for brief hours forgot and fought each other in a mighty battle, not unlike the Civil War, when brother fought brother, as they also did lately on the blood-stained poppy fields of Wales."

His audience applauded lightly.

"Did you mean to kill those union men, Mr. O'Rourke?" the reporter asked.

"No sir. That is, I never killed *no one*. I manned a Gatling gun at the mine—we call it a gat—but I never fired anywhere but well over the heads of those surrounding the mine. If this were not so, could you imagine the carnage? Me, a trained gunner in the war, and an Irish Freedom Fighter. But I have seen my share of mangled bodies, gentlemen—ladies, I apologize—and I hope never to see sights again like I seen at the Somme and Meuse-Argonne, where hundreds of human lives lay dead."

"Is it true you were shot four times, Mr. O'Rourke?"

"It is a fact that the riflemen of Southern Illinois aim true. I can vouch for the accuracy of no fewer than *eight* of their bullets."

The audience gasped.

On the floor below, a ruckus broke out, and O'Rourke reached out and held the *Evening American* man's hand, causing him to stop writing. The room hushed, and Cora peered down the stairwell to see people overflowing from the Lion's Club carnival set up outside in the street. Dr. Black shouted for them to be removed and the doors be locked, and when the silence below indicated that this had been accomplished, everyone in the hospital ward relaxed and turned back to Patrick O'Rourke.

"Thought we were going to see another fight," O'Rourke said weakly.

"Nobody's going to hurt you anymore, Mr. O'Rourke," one of the miners said. "That ain't no celebration carnival like some people are saying. We don't know who was out at that mine the other day, but that just wasn't right what they done. Most of them were from other counties, or maybe from out of state, you know how people want to get excited, and no doubt they got inflamed with liquor to do what they did. Like I said, it wasn't right, and we'll protect you with our very lives to see no further harm comes to you and your fellow scabs."

"Thank you very much, sir," O'Rourke said. "I'm really very fatigued, and I'm afraid I must rest now. Also, I wonder if someone might be so kind—seeing it's a tad hard for me to run over for myself—as to bring me some of that food that I have gotten delicious whiffs of in the past hour? I would be happy to pay a boy to...."

"Never you mind, Mr. O'Rourke," a voice from the far corner said loudly. "We'll treat you to the best dinner you've had in months, I'll bet, and I'll go out now for it myself. Be back in two shakes."

Cora stepped aside to let Mayor Marshall MacCormack out.

He began to pass but stopped. "Mrs. Sneed, what a surprise to see you here," he said. "Walk with me, won't you?"

They walked downstairs together, and the janitor let them out the door. Opposite the hospital was a lot that belonged to the Baptist Church. It was filled with people. A brass band played a polka over the struggles of a solitary accordion player and a hurdy gurdy man, whose capuchin monkey perched on his shoulder. The band had the advantage of not only numbers but also elevation and bunting. Women at different booths made of hastily-nailed lumber sold panata, zuppa di lenticchie, Italian beef sliced thin with hard rolls soaked in meat juice, lasagna, manicotti, gnocchi, spaghetti with summer tomatoes and olive oil and fresh basil, sweet ricotta pies, strufoli, and wine custard. Other women sold cornbread and greens, pies, cobblers, fresh breads, kosher meats, preserved peaches and jams, strawberries and roasted nuts. The men stood in groups talking, laughing, spitting tobacco, and drinking. There were rides and a funhouse, and children screamed and ran through the crowd holding balloons.

"Isn't it just horrible, Mrs. Sneed?" the mayor said. "I myself was out of town, but they tell me there was meanness."

"Yes, meanness," Cora said. She looked for someone she could call out to and excuse herself.

"I personally escorted seven scabs to the train. Did you know that? Mrs. Sneed?"

"No, Marshall, I didn't."

"I did. I got a call from a reporter, who said a bunch of scabs were holed up in Doc Black's examination room, and would I come and help because the mob was coming to take them away and shoot them dead."

"I thought you weren't here, Marshall."

The mayor looked confused. "No, no," he insisted. "This was later. I got my revolver from the bedside drawer and I came straight down quick as I could. There wasn't anybody around but those scabs, but I told them they had nothing to worry about, and I took them to the station and put them on the first train north. Sat there with them until it came too. That reporter was having a snow dream. That's the problem: all the reporters filed their stories from Herrin, which is only right since we've got the hotels and telegraph, but that's why everybody blames Herrin, they see that name on there, and us a city where more people own their own homes than any city I ever saw. I would have died to prevent the shedding of even one more drop of blood."

"That was a kind thing you did, Marshall," Cora said. She lay her hand on his forearm and surprised them both.

"I heard what you did defending your home, Cora," the mayor said more boldly. "A pillar of courage. Imagine those ruffians. Rednecks. Whoever they were, they had it coming. I know you wouldn't shoot any union men."

"I *did* shoot at union men, best I can remember." She smiled and tried the forearm trick again. It had the same effect on MacCormack, and she was thrilled. "And I'd shoot you too, *Mayor*, if I found you poking around *my* house." She laughed directly into his moist round face and flounced away in her black dress. He laughed uncertainly behind her.

All around the carnival men tipped their hats and women nodded as she passed. She felt she had never been well-liked, even as a child, and their acknowledgment of her nearly made her cry. These were decent men and women, she thought. And all it took was to walk among them, become involved in their lives. That too was a result of her bravery, she realized, and knew that the afternoon she had faced *men* down, on their own terms, would change everything. Her charity until then had been one-sided because they felt she condescended and so they had taken advantage of her. She had had to give them bullets with their bread to gain their respect and now things would be different.

Maybe, we said, as we watched her work through the crowd.
We had pushed when Black told us to push and screamed without permission, though we were a little embarrassed to have Mrs. Sneed there,

139

quiet and grave, already a mother to three and facing death because her latest child wouldn't be born on anybody's terms but her own. We breathed the ether and bled and cried and when we came to ourselves from twilight sleep Mrs. Sneed was still there, between contractions, buttoned to the neck and grimly holding it in. We no longer pitied her then, in fact secretly wished her harm for her properness in the pain, which we believed she brought on herself somehow. Her husband was a handsome devil, Baptist but known to dram a little bit, and we imagined him outside in his camelhair overcoat, wire spectacles, rich leather shoes, sitting at the curb in his limousine with his son-in-law chauffeur and the new gold senate star on the radiator grill, grieving for us and the work of women. Unlike our own husbands, who fell off us when they were done and began snoring like they were sawing boards down to the lumberyard. But we did love talking to each other in veiled, sly references about the making of babies almost as much as we loved the certainty of humanity inside us, and we kidded each other about never letting them stick that thing up there again, we'd become nuns first, and

that's funny, you should talk to Sister Agnes down to Saint Mary's because I heard she knows her way around the handyman's tools just fine

Oh the things you'll say

it's a lie

it's not

until Mrs. Sneed snapped from her corner, Sex is bad because it musses the bedclothes. Nurse bring the doctor. And I would remind you young ladies this is a ward not a brothel.

We waited in silence for contractions. In a moment we began to look at each other and wink and stick out our tongues and make rude finger-gestures until Amy Ritter spluttered with laughter and Mrs. Sneed threw her coverlet back and carrying her belly went to find the doctor herself. Nina Calcaterra capped it off when she said real drylike I reckon she's got herself more than a bit mussed, ain't she?

Cora hesitated to go up to the first group of women. They had been speaking in Italian but switched easily and immediately to English to include her. A Lithuanian woman, whose husband had started in the mines only days before they quit working, stood hesitantly to the side. Cora waved her to them, and they talked about the relief they felt of having

140

the hard times over and done with. The Lithuanian spoke haltingly and used her hands a lot, but they laughed their way through the difficulties together.

"Our own little League of Nations," Cora joked, and it didn't matter that most of them didn't understand. They laughed.

Cora made it a point to touch everyone—a firm handshake, a light kiss on the cheek, a hug. All this contact, she realized, was what had been missing. She knew now the role she could play and how she could step out of Will's shadow.

Everyone wanted to speak to her about what had happened at her home the day before and convey to her the many stories of local heroes aiding scabs being hunted by the mob. These good citizens hid scabs in their homes, stepped out into fields under fire to give water to the wounded, pooled their money to buy the scabs passage out of Southern Illinois. Now, they said, it's over, thank God, and there will be no more of *that*.

I heard it spread by listening on the phone.

My God, me too.

From the time they started shooting them at Harrison's Woods.

No, it was Crenshaw.

Moake Crossing.

They got it in the fields south of the Marlowe place.

I heard the American Legion wants to claim some of the scab bodies. What in the world for? Oh, and one of them was the son of the mayor of Charleston. Can you imagine?

Going to be hell to pay for that.

The women grew quiet. Cora didn't know what to say but knew equally well they were waiting for her to reassure them.

"I'm sure everything will turn out all right," she said. She felt her facial muscles stretch in imitation of a smile. There was charity in that, even grace, and her smile turned genuine. "Mr. Sneed will see to everything. We may even find ourselves in a stronger bargaining position, who knows?"

The women asked her other questions, and men came and stood casually with their hands on their wives' shoulders. They too wanted to talk, and she might have been Will for all it mattered. She expanded her views, and they still listened. More than any other sign, this sense of communal relief and newfound camaraderie meant the evil was over.

There would be a time, later, she knew, to instruct on morality and values, even to chide, but not now.

* Nearby, the bodies of the scabs had been dumped in the Dillard building, which was vacant. Joe Van Buren and the other undertaker in town, Vincent Cislaghi, helped Coroner McCown strip the bodies of their tattered clothes. Slowly, tut-tutting over the types and severity of the wounds, they washed them. The concrete turned red and became slippery with watery blood, and the two undertakers slopped pail after pail of fresh water on the floor and used push brooms to sweep the waste out over the sidewalk and into the gutter, where it ran like a thin creek the length of a block and turned the corner. Van Buren's supply of pine boxes was exhausted, as was Cislaghi's, and they begged for more from mortuaries in neighboring towns. Finally all the scabs had been cleaned, examined for the coroner's inquest, laid on the overturned pine coffins they would go into, and partly covered with white sheets. The wounds had not dried sufficiently, and stigmata rose through the sheets.

Cora left the carnival and stopped to watch Van Buren doing his work. He saw her staring. The inside of the improvised morgue was over 90 degrees, and the air didn't stir, despite the open door. The sweet stink of decay had begun.

"Mrs. Sneed," Van Buren said. He dropped his broom and wiped his hands on his apron. He was soaked with diluted blood. "Mrs. Sneed, please, you mustn't look."

Cora stood and looked. There was no novelty in nineteen dead men, and the bodies did not horrify her. They no longer looked human in the awkward way they lay on their coffin lids. The half-opened eyes, dull-glassy like marbles, and contorted mouths looked like some inferior sculptor had made a bad job of it. As she had always suspected, the sensual body was merely disgusting. She looked up at Mr. Van Buren. He was full of life, unspent, charged with possibility but trapped tending the dead day and night in his lonely mortuary. He was strong, from manhandling heavy bodies probably. Now his face showed concern—one spirit caring for another in the very presence of spirit's negation.

"Mrs. Sneed," he said, growing quieter than ever. His voice barely had the vibration to rise above a whisper.

"Mr. Van Buren."

Cora wept. In a way she could not later remember, he turned out to be holding her tightly against his chest. She felt her dress dampen with the blood-water from his clothes, and when she finally pulled herself away—he was not holding her against her will, after all—she expected to be covered with gore, but her black clothing showed only a slight dampness.

Quickly, word spread through the community that the bodies were ready for display, and Herrinites began to arrive singly and in pairs. Later the extended families, moving more slowly, and out-of-towners came. Cora stood near the door and watched them for an hour then stepped back as the visitors' faces became less familiar and the odor of the dead rose. Iridescent green horseflies began to buzz around the screened windows and flew in the open door to cluster on the scabs' eyes and open wounds. The visitors spit in the faces of the dead and spoke to them, saying things like, "You're one son-of-a-bitch that won't hurt my babies anymore. Will you. Will you."

Van Buren, his work done for the moment, found Cora sitting on the curb near the church.

"Have you been praying?" he asked.

Cora looked at him and shook her head.

"Many of the bodies have been claimed," he said. "People out east, from up north. They'll be taken care of and given a decent burial."

"What about the others?"

"Jordie and Joe will get the works, all paid for by the union. They're having Jordie's funeral at Charles Green's house. I think he and Jordie served together. There's another union man from Marion, Guy Hudgens, was stomach-shot last night. He's not in much pain yet, but I expect he'll die."

"I meant the non-union men's bodies that aren't claimed."

Van Buren shook his head. "There's UMW men out in the potter's field now digging sixteen graves."

"How did we come to this?" Cora said. She had Will in mind when she asked the question, and she was surprised when Van Buren answered.

"Too many people want too many things." He looked down on the part in Cora's hair, where her scalp showed white like the scar of a healed cut. "On the other hand, it's a mystery, don't you think?"

"It has to stop," Cora said. "We must make it stop."

Will did not come home that day. The next morning Cora, eager for more freedom to see and be seen, asked Lena House to watch the children again so she could go out. In town she passed shop windows with hand-printed cards saying that Jordie Henderson and Joe Pitkewicius would be buried Sunday, and everyone who loved the union and what it stood for should attend. She thought of how she should represent Will at the funerals. She was sure he would want her to do so. She wanted to.

On the way home she stopped at Bailey's for candy for the kids and the day's papers. Mr. Bailey stood in the telegrapher's booth with a crazed look. He waved at her and told her to take anything she wanted on account. He had been deluged, he said, with messages from across the United States and had not taken a break since breakfast. People were asking if it was true that seventy-five innocents had been brutally murdered and five women cut into little pieces. Bailey planned to leave by midnight even if there was work left to do.

The papers described the early backlash. President Harding had called a cabinet meeting on "the problem in Williamson County." The Governor of Illinois said he didn't think the stories could be true, but if they were it was all the fault of the Attorney General, who had kept the governor away from his duties on trumped-up charges of fraud and embezzlement. He'd had to rely on his men to handle the situation, and it had gotten out of hand. Cora read all the papers as she drank coffee and watched the girls play next door through the window. Black Jack Pershing wanted to march on Herrin, and the Assistant Secretary of the Navy, Colonel Teddy Roosevelt, Jr., vented his outrage at the atrocities.

The first list of destroyed property had been drawn by Bull, Lytton and Olson, of Chicago, exposed by their suit against Williamson County filed on behalf of the coal company. Evidently $217,420 in Bucyrus shovels, a team of horses with wagon and harness, buildings, tools, compressors, a steam pump, maps, record books and documents were missing or destroyed. This was the same firm that represented the men who had escaped; their claims were for clothes, jewelry, luggage and other items to be disclosed, at an average value of $250 to $1,000 each.

Senator Myers of Montana, an old labor foe, said that what had happened in Herrin was "more horrible, more shocking, and more inexcusable than any German atrocity in the war." That had given one mine owner the idea that the union should be sued for exactly one million dollars.

According to a related article, another scene had taken place only yesterday afternoon, outside West Frankfort, a few miles to the north. When four "Mexicans" were found walking along railroad tracks there, a crowd formed and chased them—solely to ask if they were refugees from the Lester Mine massacre and if they needed help. The crowd had run down two of the men and taken them to jail, for their own safety, the paper said. A third man escaped but the fourth recklessly climbed a coal chute. When local men went up to get him he jumped to the tracks below and broke his neck. His death had been ruled "suicide due to fright."

Of course other union men were found shot too. Jim Morris of Johnston City got his in the left arm. Guy Hudgens had indeed been shot in the stomach. "It is believed his wounds will prove fatal," the paper said. Cora winced at the thought of the wounded man reading the paper or being read to. He would die, of course, but it would take a good long while, and he would be in considerable pain.

Like boys, Cora thought, still playing silly games. Women knew better by the age of ten. Honestly.

Will was different. She could look at him and forget he was a man sometimes. Strange, and she would never say it to him, but he was kind, thoughtful. Gentle, like a woman. This business had the potential to destroy him, and she was determined to save him from himself at any cost. She would bear any burden, martyr herself if necessary to keep sanity in her home. The children must have it, and Will deserves it, she thought. Such a hard life. Just a child and already down in the mines, breathing the gas and lying in freezing oily water, swinging a pick. And then making something of himself, day by day, all those years. Endurance was surely the greatest of his gifts. But again, funny how you could look at him in his suit and hat, sitting in the back of the car, and believe he had never done manual labor, that he was weak, even. The look of intelligence on him, which could be mistaken for something else, and his fleshy laborer hands hidden deep in his pockets. She had thought of him when she read that poetess:

The Props assist the House
Until the House is built
And then the Props withdraw
And adequate, erect,
The House support itself
And cease to recollect
The Auger and the Carpenter—
Just such a retrospect
Hath the perfected Life—
A past of Plank and Nail
And slowness—then the Scaffolds drop
Affirming it a Soul.

To recollect the carpenter would be to dwell on something that wasn't the dwelling. He was a lesser form of American aristocracy, and if he could keep the will—funny how Will needed will or he would not be Will—who knew where it might all lead? She slid her hands down her sides and doubted she was good enough.

She thought about going across the alley to pick up her children from Lena, since she needed to be close now. She noticed Mr. Van Buren letting himself into the front door of his business. She started to call to him but Will had painted the windows shut on that side of the kitchen. She trotted for the back door, changed her mind and ran to the front and called his name, but Van Buren had gone inside. She stole across the street and tapped on his door with her nails.

"Mrs. Sneed. How nice. Is there trouble? Can I help?"

"No, please, I just wanted to see if...can I get you anything to eat? You must have had an awfully long day. Or can you not eat after...a job like yours must be draining, Mr. Van Buren." She laughed and covered her mouth.

"I am used to it, Mrs. Sneed, and I find I always have an appetite."

"Mr. Van Buren, please, we've been neighbors for ten years. Call me Cora."

"And you must call me Joe."

"Sure, Joe. What would you like? What do you like to eat? I can fix something in an instant."

146

"Oh no, you mustn't. It's too much of a bother. I have some cheese and some bread. I'll make do."

"Don't be silly," Cora said. "You can't survive on bread, you'll make yourself sick. Let me go across the way and fix you something to eat, and I'll bring it back shortly. Okay?" she asked. "Is that okay? Please, I want to."

"Okay, Cora," Van Buren said tightly. He held her gaze and then looked away. "Will you join me though? Have you eaten? Bring enough for us both, and I'll clear my table so we can eat together."

Cora was excited and happy and realized only after she had returned to her house that she had nothing to feed him. She wished she had learned to drive, it would have been quicker, but the car was still with the mechanic anyway, she remembered, and suddenly thought: poor Will. She took money from the cookie jar and started for the nearest market. For no good reason she didn't want Lena or Joe to see her going to that trouble, so she walked in the opposite direction for a block, went east another block, then turned toward Pasquali's. She knew this would take time, so she hurried.

When she returned the same way, she was sweating and nearly forty-five minutes had passed. Working quickly she seasoned some chicken, rolled it in flour, put it in a smoking pan to fry, and started a pot of rice. Both the chicken and the rice seemed to take forever, and she knew she was making them cook slower by poking at them constantly. Finally, they were mostly done, and she put dishes, a loaf of fresh Italian bread, and a jug of lemonade in a basket. She took the meal to the funeral home, rang the bell, and turned her back to the door, fluffing her wet hair and stretching her back under her dress.

"Mrs. Sneed, how kind."

"Mr. Van Buren."

They laughed at their silliness. Joe ushered her back through the visitation room, now empty, through a storeroom stacked on both sides with boxes, and down a hallway lighted by a small window set very high in the wall. The air smelled like dust, but not like decay, embalming fluid, or calla lilies, as she had half-feared. At the back of the house was a kitchenette with a sink, a burner, and a battered wooden table with two loose-limbed chairs. Joe had placed a silk arrangement there as a centerpiece. Cora had seen it dozens of times on the table in front where

147

guests signed the visitation books.

"I just brought fried chicken," she said. "I'm sorry, you probably don't like it."

"Oh yes, I do."

"It's not what you're used to, I'm sure."

Joe smiled. "I love fried chicken, and you're right. I don't get to have it as often as I'd like."

"I'm sorry. I didn't mean anything by that," she said, meaning his ethnicity.

"I get by just fine," Joe said, referring to his bachelorhood. "I'm sorry I don't have anything to add to this. Oh, wait. Let's start with an aperitif. Would you care for a Campari and soda?"

"I've never tried it," Cora said. "Let's have one."

Later, after their lunch, Joe showed her the ground floor of his home, apologizing for how much of it was taken over by his business.

"Very practical," Cora said. "You know, my cousin bought a coffin for her husband here. She said you were very kind."

"Thank you. I do try to be, Cora. Loss is always upsetting, and sometimes people don't have someone to help them through it, even when they have family."

"You're so right. I know that myself."

They had come to a room on the north side of the house where it was cool and dark. The room had been designed for some other use, Cora knew. It reminded her of Will's library, but instead of books it was filled with caskets. The moldings, cornices, and the rosette on the ceiling helped to make the room seem overstuffed, though there was no furniture except, well, the final kind, and she didn't know what to say.

"Are these the latest models?" she said.

"Yes, people are beginning to want more for their kin these days. Comes with progress, I suppose, and I'm thankful."

"Don't you think it's odd, though? No offense, Joe. But all this wasted velvet and brass? I'm sorry, it's your trade. But when I go…. If no one says it for me, and you're the one taking care of me, be sure no one goes overboard with all this mess."

"I know, Cora. I think of that too. It's cynical to say, but I won't have anything fancy at all. I'll give you what I want myself."

"So you've picked yours out?" She laughed.

148

"I haven't decided," Van Buren said. He smiled. "But I have tried out a few of them."

"What do you mean?" Cora said with mock horror.

"Lain in them. Just to see."

"To see what? How awful."

"Aren't you the tiniest bit curious?"

"Never in a million years. It's the strangest thing I ever heard."

"Maybe you wouldn't have done it. I can't say I ever would have, except they're here, and I work around them every day; they're both nothing to me and everything. I wanted to be able to tell my customers which ones were better. Surely you would have done the same if you were me. Please, don't make me feel bad about it."

"I'm sorry, Joe. I wasn't trying to be mean. I was just teasing. I don't see anything wrong with it at all."

"Would you like to try one now?"

"No! Don't they say if you lie down in one you'll soon be in it for good?"

"I've never heard that superstition," Van Buren said. He grinned. "Of course, it would take courage to do this."

"Was that a challenge?" Cora said. "I think maybe you're daring me to something, Mr. Van Buren. You think I don't have the guts to do it."

"Do you?" he said, a high school boy talking to a girl again. "Do you? Bet you don't. I'll bet you a cup of coffee you don't."

"All right then," Cora said. "Just to show you that a Sneed can do anything," she said, instantly regretting the mention of her last name.

She stepped up on the low dais on which the elaborate gilt coffin sat, swirled her skirt around her with one hand and pulled herself over the edge of the box. She hurt her bottom, when she fell backward into it, and realized the plush-looking quilted interior was a sham. A panic rose in her when she also realized that with her knees up she wouldn't be able to get the momentum to lift herself out and that her friend Joe was helping her turn so she could lie down and go through with their little bet. He supported the back of her neck and lifted under her knees, laying her in the coffin and arranging her body the way he had so many others. His body, radiating heat through his clothes, loomed over her like a closing lid, and as she struggled to sit up, she found that he was holding her down with one hand tightly gripping the hair at the base of her skull, the other at the curve of her waist, as his face came down to her cold, fearful lips.

CHAPTER SEVENTEEN

She did not hear Will come in. He had returned the car to Van Buren's garage and walked home across the street with his bag in hand. She turned from her dressing table and saw him standing in the doorway, imposing, large, male. She smiled hopefully.

He stood gazing down on her as if his mood had yet to be formed then dropped his bag with a thud when her smile decided it.

"The house okay?" he asked. He did not approach, let alone touch her.

"The house?"

"Yes, the house, the children. You. Is everyone okay? It's not a difficult question."

"We're fine. Are you tired?"

He nodded and looked around as if he wanted to be doing something else.

"Can I fix you something?"

"Food is the last thing I want."

"A cool drink?"

"No."

He stripped his collar and shirt. His chest was beginning to sag, and he had a belly. He looked thick through the trunk, skinny in the arms, and very pale.

"Cora...."

She started to go to him, but he held her at bay with his palm. She turned back to her dressing table and put her hair up as she waited.

He waited until the emotion, whatever it was, passed.

"You hate me, don't you?" he asked.

She nearly swallowed the hairpin between her lips. "Hate you? Will, what are you saying?"

"It doesn't matter." He began unpacking his suitcase.

They worked separately. Cora could hear the grandfather clock on the first floor ticking. She prayed it was not near the hour; the chime would have been too much.

"Will, you must know I'll always love you, no matter what."

"No reason that can't include hatred," he said.

"You make no sense. You and the children are the most important things in my life, and nothing will ever change that. You're loved, and that's all."

She looked out the bedroom window. Across the street, in his own bedroom, Mr. Van Buren was changing to go out. He looked up and saw her looking. His suspenders hung at his sides, and his shirt was not tucked into his pants. He opened his mouth as if to say something. Cora lifted her hand and motioned. He waved back. She pulled the shade the rest of the way down.

"You think it was wrong for me to leave, don't you?" Will said.

"I'm the one told you to leave. Remember?"

"And why would you do that?" He threw his suitcase into the back of the closet. Clothing on hangers and the shoes beneath them broke the case's fall, so it didn't make as much noise as he intended.

Cora said, "Because I am looking out for you and our children and the town. Our only hope now—for any of us—is for you to lead the way out."

"There is no way out of what happened. You can't know."

"Perhaps. But there will be murder trials, and you can't be one of the defendants. If you were, more than your career would fall."

"You think I'm a coward," he accused her suddenly. He took a step in her direction and raised his voice. The intensity in his eyes scared her.

"Do you think somehow I would respect you more if you had slaughtered innocent men promised safe passage out of this town? You can't believe that." She felt herself judging him as he seemed to demand. She did think he was weak, but only because he was afraid of her judgment. She felt sick at heart that some important piece of him had failed, collapsed like the floor of a burnt house, but it also brought to mind her own strength.

151

"How many people on this earth care for you the way I do, Will, the way the children do? Think of the millions of souls on this earth right now and how, nearly to a man, no one knows either of us exist. Of those who do, how many actually love you, apart from what you'll do for them? Ten people? How many would suffer for you in the same way that you're willing to sacrifice your life to them? How many would even do without something to make you more comfortable? We are everything you have, Will. Why in the world do you insist on loving beyond your family? Look at me. Look at me now." She went to him aggressively.

They were both surprised, and the sudden shock of contact made them hungry. As she lay under him she thought, excitedly, he's thinking of some little whore as he roughs me up. Cora took his hand and placed it at the nape of her neck and closed his fist around her hair.

"Look at me," she said. "Look into my eyes."

He lost himself in her eyes, so close they were blurry and a multitude, and wondered sadly how she came to think of new tricks after so many years.

Afterwards they were embarrassed and purposefully tender. He got up for water, and she went to the bathroom.

"When did you start keeping Campari in the house?" he called to her. "Who gave you that idea?"

She came in dressed and straightened. "Why would someone have to give me the idea?" she asked. "Can't I just try new things?"

He intuited that some aspect of power had shifted and wondered if that was how a woman acted who had found out that her husband had mistresses, or one who despised him for leaving when he'd been needed at home. Maybe she hated him but loved the idea of his office.

There was little else to say, and the day was unhappy.

All weekend we waited. We knew America's burgeoning middle class with their bourgeois attitudes would not understand the importance of what we'd done. They didn't know that scabs were like cancer: if one got a toehold, he multiplied endlessly and nullified all the hard-won battles for the rights of man. But no one praised us for doing our part. No one in the country even came to our defense. Even the national union stayed silent.

On Sunday, Cora told Will she wanted to go with him to the funerals. He seemed surprised but said he was glad. They attended Jordie Henderson's funeral first. Charles Green's home was not far, so they walked. As they got closer, the streets were lined with autos, and so many people trotted toward the funeral so fervently that it felt as if they were walking up for a game at Wrigley. Cora made it to the front porch and no further, while Will pushed in to see Jordie's casket. It was closed because of his face. Cora listened to Reverend Lee eulogize Jordie and tried to count the people surrounding the two-bedroom house in a neighborhood of two-bedroom houses with young oaks in the lawns. There were so many she gave up at a thousand, and she figured that was only a quarter of the crowd. Boys and men filled the forks and branches of every tree capable of supporting their weight. It took nearly an additional hour for the white hearse to be loaded, the twenty-piece band to assemble at the head of the column, and mourners to line up. Pallbearers walked next to the hearse as it crept in the direction of the cemetery. Bullyrag Greathouse was one of them, and he waved cheerfully at Cora. Two thousand union men, union women, union children and dogs followed on foot. The automobiles in the procession strung out for an entire mile, and the hearse arrived at the cemetery before the last of the cars had left Charles Green's place.

Reporters on the scene, both local and national, were met with a sullen silence that cracked open with a few questions, to the newsmen's delight.

> We are not drunken mobs, infuriated foreigners, anarchists, bolsheviki or any of the other unjust and uncalled-for things that the media have charged us with. We are a 100% American community that resented the importation of thugs and gunmen from the slums of Chicago. The situation is just that of the Boston Tea Party, and if King George seems like a stretch, then WJ Lester is like Kaiser Wilhelm, who started a worldwide war.

Joe Pitkewicius had his chance later that day, and even though he was Catholic, Baptist and Presbyterian ministers ran the show with the priest in the background doing the work of blessings. The pallbearers were fellow members of the Herrin Lithuanian Lodge. This time, Cora stayed behind and watched the procession leave for the cemetery. She counted eighty automobiles, not as many as Jordie had, and the mourners didn't look as upset. Maybe the earlier funeral tired them, or Jordie being a Scot had something to do with it.

Will had to excuse himself from the procession when he caught wind that Fox Hughes and several citizens of Herrin were meeting at the Ly-Mar Hotel to draft a wire to President Harding about the derogatory press they had received, due not in small part to the president himself. By the time he got there, the telegram was already taking shape: "Leader of democracy dare not stifle workers' struggle. Stop. Federal control of mines cannot be. Stop. Citizens of this region want to do right thing but if more scabbing occurs we cannot be held responsible for what might happen. Stop." The committee had had too many drinks to remember Joe Pitkewicius' funeral and didn't notice when it passed on the street.

As Cora was walking home alone on Park Avenue she was passed by two identical trucks carrying pine coffins, two-wide and four-high, held down by cargo straps. The scabs, she realized. Those men. She felt a lonely chill.

A young woman was waiting on the front steps to Cora's house.

It was the first visit by Shelley Brown to her home, she would often think later, but then have to correct herself every time. She had seen the girl before, when there was a disagreement over pay and the mother had brought her daughter with her to make a point and try to shame Cora. Cora had held it against both of them but retracted her feelings when she'd heard they were so obviously distraught at the funeral of Shelley's father. Mrs. Brown had charged the casket, wailing, and tried to pull her husband from it. Shelley helped restrain her, though she was just a girl. A girl, but developed, and aware of it.

Now she was a young woman, not a girl, and her eyes held secret knowledge, and Cora was afraid again on the steps to her own home.

"You are Mrs. Brown's daughter."

The girl nodded her head and looked down.

"Please come in."

"Mrs. Sneed." The girl sat and hugged her own knees.

"I said come in."

They went inside then, the silence between them complete. Cora watched the girl cautiously. She ushered her to a stool in the kitchen and made coffee. They stayed quiet. The girl did not appear to be ill at ease whatsoever being in Cora's house, just miserable. Cora thought back, trying to find some time when the girl might have been there when she herself had not been home. She hurt somewhere but couldn't say where it was. The idea that the woman was not a whore disturbed her. She had not thought Will could love someone else when he had his family. She felt silly, naïve, like a child, in the presence of this other woman half her age. She looked at the girl and thought of the difference in their emotional lives. Cora could not remember being twenty, or what it felt like. She wanted to laugh the way she had laughed at Mayor MacCormack but also to cry at the thought that she was old enough to be Shelley's mother. Each of the feelings led off the scale, she knew, but together they held her in suspension.

She poured the coffee and added lots of cream and sugar without asking. "There," she said. "Now you'd better tell me. Is it a child? Money for a child or not to have a child?"

Shelley looked up, and Cora studied her. Her skin was relatively light, and her hair had been straightened. Cora wondered what colored men thought of her, and why she couldn't stick to them. Will, of course, was to blame for he'd gone through with it even though he was older, married, and powerful. And he picked a type that Cora herself was not—beautiful—which heightened the betrayal. Still she didn't hate him as much as she did her.

Shelley paused, and Cora hoped she would not sit here in her home and lie to her face. Or maybe she hoped she would. Cora began her first internal check as to what she was capable of doing if the girl lied.... The girl did appear to consider it, or her hesitancy made it seem so, but she came to the point instead.

"Mrs. Sneed, it's my brother. He's gone missing, and there are rumors he was involved in the killings. These white men, they might walk away, but Jeremy.... They'll kill Jeremy just to make themselves feel better about what they've done."

"I see. You're here.... I thought you wanted to speak to me. Mr. Sneed is at the funeral now."

"But I did want to talk to you. Bill—Mr. Sneed—can move as slow or fast as he wants. I was hoping, getting to meet you, talking to you, that I could convince you that I am not a demon, or that I've done anything to ruin what you have. Bill does love you. He tells me."

155

"You've discussed it?" Cora's anger rose. "Is there a child or not?"

"No, Mrs. Sneed, I'm not pregnant. I thought a few months ago that I was, but if I was I miscarried so early I couldn't be sure. Now I know I'm not."

"I see. How long has it been this way?"

"How long has Bill been seeing me? In the way you'd care, six months. He started being kind is all, and that's been going on a long time. He's kind to everyone. He is a good man."

"I know Mr. Sneed better than he knows himself. Shelley, you couldn't expect I'd be happy to help you."

"Can't you see by that how desperate I am? I'm here despite my shame. You think I ever felt I had the rights to Bill that you do? Or that I feel sly in carrying on? Mrs. Sneed, please. I need your help."

"I'm tempted to ask what you'll do for me," Cora said. "What did you plan to promise me in exchange for this favor?"

The girl looked down again, and Cora sobered. Shelley had not come to exchange Will for her brother after all.

"What has Will promised you?" Cora asked gently.

"Nothing. It's not like that. But he does have a weak spot for people depending on him."

"You love him?"

"No."

Cora saw she lied and couldn't bear it. "He's given you money? Promised trips? Gifts and things for your home?"

"Mrs. Sneed, please."

"Goddamn it all, you may as well call me Cora."

The girl smiled for the first time. "Cora, he just represents a better life."

"Monetarily?"

"No. That will be part of it, or would have been, eventually. But not for me. For Jeremy. Bill already got him made a deputy out in Colp. I've heard how he helps people all over with a call, a letter. My brother is very smart and could be anything he wanted to be."

Cora sat with her forearms bracketing a cup of cooling coffee in the quiet commanded by the grandfather clock in the next room. She hesitated to go along, unsure of what she would lose if she did so.

"What do you want, girl?" she said finally.

"Bill...."

"Please call him Mr. Sneed in my presence," Cora said. "It helps. I know it's just a trick, but it helps. Call me Cora, and him Mr. Sneed."

"I want Mr. Sneed to find my brother and get us moved somewhere safe, far from here. I'd like Jeremy to have a chance at being a professional man."

"Some sort of lay-doctor? Or the clergy?"

"I don't care. Even a lawyer would be good enough."

"And you think Will has this power?" Cora asked. She was interested in the answer and for some reason trusted the girl's judgment.

"Yes ma'am, I do. He's spoken of similar cases. Granted, they weren't colored men, but yes. I do believe."

"I see." Cora paused, aware again, for the second time recently—she couldn't remember the first—of Bill's power reflecting on her. "But why didn't you ask him yourself?"

"He's angry with Jeremy."

"Many will be. And there are dangers he's let himself in for, your brother.... How far would you have to go to get what you want? Herrin is not Boston, as you know."

"All the way out of America, if we had to. Bill—Mr. Sneed—would know where."

"If there is an ocean between you and Mr. Sneed, you may call him Bill," Cora said. She smiled, and the girl did too, but it made Cora angry.

"Is there a place you can go now where Will cannot find you?" Cora said. "I cannot do what you ask with your interference. And I won't do it if you don't agree."

"Yes," the girl said. "I have family." She clutched her own arms, Cora realized, to keep from springing forward, and the thought of making contact with the little whore sickened and frightened her for the absolute reality it represented.

"Then go there. Leave me your address. That's in Franklin County? Yes, I know that area. It's where Will was born. He didn't tell you? You go there and wait for me to call for you. It may be a few days."

She looked Shelley over closely, almost threateningly. "I won't do you wrong, girl. But you have to expect I'll get something from this too. So you wait. And when I send for you, come and do exactly as I say. If you do otherwise, I think you know what will happen."

157

"I can imagine it."

"I'm madder at him than I am at you right now. Don't make me that mad at you."

"Cora. I've thought how we're...similar. Wait. I don't mean with Mr. Sneed. I mean that together we're the secret part of this town that gets whispered in all those voices...."

Cora blushed with rage.

"...but it doesn't matter because it's never the whole story. Same thing out at that mine. Nobody knew anybody truly. That's why it happened."

"You're a Pollyanna, girl," Cora said. "Nearly ridiculous, I would say. If your brother was involved, I damn him for the troubles he'll cause this town, just as I curse you for what you did to my family. But he doesn't deserve to be the scapegoat in this business just because he's colored any more than you deserve to be mistreated because Will is a satyr."

Cora held back a smile at the girl's discomfort. Shelley had not touched her coffee.

"Please don't put a curse on me," Shelley said.

"I figure if the Lord Jesus Christ can forgive adultery and fornication, I can too. Eventually, maybe. Here."

Cora opened a jar and pulled out a few bills. She lay them on the table in front of the girl. Shelley did not touch or even look at them. Cora looked for something else and found chicken left from her meal with Van Buren.

"Take this too," she said. "You can nibble it as you're headed out to your relatives' place." She marveled at feeding one who had wronged her so greatly. What a strange decision.

"I love my brother," Shelley said.

"I know. Now go on. I'll send for you."

Cora escorted her out through the parlor and off the porch. The girl walked steadily, shamelessly, head-up and chest-out down the sidewalk toward town. Cora stood in the shade on the porch and watched her, as if to make sure she didn't double back and sneak in the house. Little hussy. Witch. Her mind caved again under the weight of conflicting emotions and disjointed thoughts. All this evil about, yet she could feel a primitive, senseless, appreciative joy in her new knowledge, and she did not intend to waste it.

CHAPTER EIGHTEEN

While the indictments were underway Bully went poking around the abandoned Lester mine for loot. There wasn't much left, some wire he might sell, a copper kettle, a smashed generator too big to move without a truck and the help of several men, a bunch of old shoes and boots. The boxcars had burned down to their trucks, all the windows were shot out on the sheds, and there were patches of blood-soaked dirt and some teeth underfoot. Two hopper cars of coal that Lester had intended to ship to market were still burning and would continue to do so for the next week. He found Jeremy Brown hiding on the property.

"You the boy cut those throats?" Bully said but softened when he saw Jeremy's face. "Remind me not to hire you if I want something done right."

"I did enough," Jeremy boasted.

"You better hope not. They'll hang you for just one success."

"They'll never catch me. My sister and I are getting out of here. She's been planning it for a long time, I think. I don't know. I didn't used to be real interested, I guess."

"That's good," Bully said. "Because *that* ain't gonna happen." He sensed that the boy's corrupt, halfhearted ambitions had been fed to him.

"Oh yes it is. Bill Sneed promised."

"Right. Thought so. I'm sure then."

"What do you mean by that?"

"Nothing. Look, my opinion's not worth anything, but I don't think it matters what you did or didn't do. My feeling is you'll be all right."

"You think so?" Jeremy said.

159

"Lot of people had a hand in what went on out here."

Bully and Jeremy hid in the trees on the far side of the mine when the Commission showed up to look for a mass grave a witness claimed to have seen. The men were out of their cars for half an hour, smoking and talking. They kicked the dust several times, peered into the pit, and left.

Jeremy was relieved and in a humorous mood. He pointed to the roll of wire Bully had scavenged.

"You going to use that to keep your wife home from now on?" he asked.

Bully just snorted and shook his head. He was realizing he was smarter and better than he had thought. Certainly better than Sally, or could have been if only he'd thought to resist her garden variety of evil sooner. He marveled that he hadn't. People's ability to work on him in different ways had always made him think they were smarter than they were. And, strangely, he had believed smart was the same as good, so he'd followed blindly. Now he'd set things right, he vowed. Now he'd leave Sally for good. She was nothing but a murderer. An unfaithful, manipulative, stupid, unimaginative, showy *public* murderer.

CHAPTER NINETEEN

Shelley didn't go to her relatives as she'd promised, but Bill Sneed didn't come looking either and that made her uneasy. She didn't want to miss the grand jury and each night read again in the papers what she'd seen that day. They called it the biggest murder trial in US history and the trial of the century, since the century was now nearly a quarter-gone and it was hard to imagine anything bigger happening.

One of the papers said the jury looked worse than the accused. That was good, Shelley thought. Damn. Bunch of string-bean farmers and miners worn down to the nub, unshaven and as dirty as if they'd come straight from the fields and pits to sit in judgment.

Seventy-four were indicted in all, including Hugh Willis, District Executive Board member, and others in elected positions, such as the union's sub-district secretary-treasurer, an office that Bill Sneed had once held.

The papers quoted us to show how unrepentant we were:

> *The Grand Jury report was written by the attorney general in collaboration with the Illinois Chamber of Commerce, all known labor-haters. They never shed a tear for hardworking union miners, only for men who gave their addresses at Chicago flophouses. The AG works for whoever's putting up the money, the way he did in the East St. Louis riots, otherwise he won't lift a hand. And the Chamber wants to break our morale, take little children out of school before their time, give less food to the wives and children of workers.*

161

That rascal Larry Jansen told a man from the *New York Times*, "We live in *America*, brother. It don't matter what the truth is, long as you have a good lawyer. I'm just going to enjoy myself though all this."

In fact all of Little Egypt enjoyed the proceedings so thoroughly that the judge had to have the old seating in the courtroom ripped out and new furniture put in to accommodate audiences, and even then people stood outside the courthouse calling to those in the doorway to tell them what was going on. When the workmen tore up the old jury booth they found empty whiskey bottles underneath, and the out-of-town newsmen got a kick out of that too.

As revenge for all the bad press, local news vendors stopped selling out-of-town papers in their shops, and readers who wanted to see how the rest of the world viewed the proceedings had to step in through the back of the newsstands and say the right words.

Shelley checked all the jails for Jeremy. In the county jail in Marion several dozen indicted miners played cards, sang and told stories to pass the time. Their leader there, as he had been on the march, was Otis Clark. His wife brought chicken dinners that the other men praised so highly that every wife and girlfriend and mother of the accused wanted to be the one to make chicken dinners that day, and Otis had to use his organizational skills to plan the logistics of mealtimes. Some old man from Harrisburg brought up five pounds of honey from his own hives and two pounds of sweet butter for their biscuits. Shelley wished Jeremy could get in on that.

Boredom set in for accused and observer alike, relieved only when UMW lawyers brought in new men who turned themselves in voluntarily. Miners all over the state pledged one percent of their earnings to defend them while pro-business forces built a financial war chest for the trials. Shelley sat on the town square between sessions in hopes Jeremy would appear. She knew it looked strange, a pretty young colored girl in a print dress and wide-brimmed hat, sitting on a bench alone while the white men in their denim shirts and coveralls smoked on the other five benches or at the base of the clock tower in the middle of the square. She could have guessed the time by how they moved to avoid the sun as they whittled and spit. She felt safe enough but dreaded the change when she was linked to her brother.

During one of the afternoon sessions Shelley heard the legal machinations and complications resulting from various eyewitnesses to the massacre. Don Black, a newsman from Chicago, testified on the stand that he had tried to give water to the injured as they lay dying in the Herrin cemetery, but the mob had made him pour his bucket of water on the ground. That was after he saw a colored man cut throats, one-by-one. He wasn't sure he could identify him. Shelley, standing at the back of the crowd, broke into sobs and was pulled away by Wallace Duncan, who had come out of nowhere.

He got her outside and put her against the brick wall, held her up against it roughly or reassuringly—hard to tell with that big-ass white boy with his thick neck and calm, flat eyes—and told her to stop worrying. Wallace had talked to somebody who'd seen Jeremy hiding in a rabbit hole near the Lester mine property. Mr. Sneed had sent Wallace out to talk to him and very generously offered Jeremy the services of the UMW legal team even though Jeremy wasn't a miner.

"Your brother's a hardhead, Shelley," Wallace said. "Says he's not coming in except on his own terms, when he's good and ready. I admire his spunk, but that boy's going to wind up swinging at the end of a rope. Whether he comes in or not, you aren't doing him any good bawling in front of all these people. Mr. Sneed suggests you stay home this week, and he'll come see you soon as Jeremy's in safe."

Shelley returned the next morning to hear more. Sneed was sitting in the front row with his head down as witnesses described his car pulling up to the line of scabs as they were marched away from the mine, and how "The President" ordered the killings. The prosecutor asked the witness if the man he was describing was present in the courtroom and looked at Sneed leadingly. But the witness looked around carefully and answered no, and Shelley let her breath out in relief, even a kind of pride.

Two days later she was there again when Jeremy walked into the courtroom to give himself up, carrying Bill's suit jacket draped over one arm. Bill was in his usual spot taking notes and looked up startled at Jeremy's touch. Jeremy handed him the jacket. Bill stared at it uncomprehendingly then scowled. Even as Jeremy was being taken into custody, Bill slapped at the dirt and went through the breast pockets. His face twisted in disbelief when he came across his speech written for that day—an eternity ago—at the union hall. Shelley remembered how Jeremy was to give Bill some message from her. What had it been about? She rushed forward to her brother, but the bailiff pushed her back sharply. She turned on Bill.

"You people get Jeremy back here only to crucify him?"

Bill held up the sheets of his speech spotted with bloody fingerprints and re-inspected the dark patches on his coat. He looked up at Shelley accusingly, and she had to pause. But it was Sneed's coat, after all, and his bloody words. Let him swing from the gibbet.

Sneed, still unable to speak, stood and looked down on her.

Shelley knew to keep still but couldn't. "Do something for him," she cried. "You promised. You said you would."

Sneed stared and Shelley knew she had given away her connection to his wife. He took his coat and papers and walked out through the gallery with the crowd looking at him. Shelley ran after him.

"Bill, you promised. You have to keep your word."

Sneed kept walking, ignoring her, and she raised her voice.

"Help him!"

Sneed walked out of the building into the sun and strode away.

"You bastard," she called from the front steps, just loud enough, and a couple of miners turned to see what was happening. Jeremy would hang for the awful, sinful things he'd done that were instigated by the very society that hated him for his color. Shelley felt her certainty in God's justice tremble as in an earthquake.

The prosecution did work in earnest to hang somebody, but the trials began with white miners and it was in the best interest of the whole community that no one be singled out for any action taken on that day, not even Jeremy Brown. The hot air from the couple of pedestal-mounted fans near the judge's bench didn't reach Shelley, though their roar made it hard to follow the talking, talking, motions, none of it prosecution or defense. Shelley got there early enough one morning to get a seat for a change, but Wallace stood next to her and cupped his hand from the waist, indicating she should get up and come with him. Shelley ignored him and fanned her face with a sheet of paper. Wallace bent and whispered, "You want Mr. Sneed should know about East St. Louis?"

Shelly's stomach churned. "Tell Bill Sneed I hope he rots in hell."

Wallace grinned and shook his head but left her alone. He'd always been kind to her and had once said when he got enough money to quit the force he was going to buy a saloon and let her run the kitchen. He wasn't such a bad guy. Just worked for one.

Five hundred thousand dollars was raised for bond and defense by the Sohns, Del'Eras, Stotlars, Herrins, Oldanis, Borens, Marlows and Jacks, all the oldest names in town. Shelley read the newspapers more avidly all the time. Only eight men were denied bail, including Jeremy Brown, colored.

There has been a coroner's jury, a grand jury, and now a trial. At the end of the coroner's jury, the jury, mostly union miners, shook hands with the indicted cheerfully and wished them all well. One supposes things will not change for the trial, now underway with the first five of the defendants, wearing clean collars. They were closely shaved, and to pass the time they chewed gum and chatted with each other. I have never seen jurors look tougher than the prisoners, but this part of the state is that way, and they are just a segment of the community on trial.

Otis Clark is the leader and most intelligent of them. About 40 years old, he has a strong nose and jaw. He is a champion checker player—this reporter has lost several games to him—and he says he has sold insurance, been a carpenter, a miner, and a farmer. He is from one of the pioneer families. His father went for the union when the county was split between rebs and union and might have gone either way. Otis was building a house in Weaver when he was arrested on his ladder; the carpenters union is finishing the job while he rests.

Bert Grace, on the other hand, is a natty dresser and looks more like a prosperous salesman. He told me he's not a member of any radical organization at all, not even the Elks or Rotarians. He asked me to find out how his motor at the mine is doing, and the jailer told me Grace wants out so badly that they had to put him in a private cell.

Leva Mann is slow, quiet-spoken, with a pleasant southern drawl that brings to mind the tobacco fields of Kentucky. He is grave, sorrowful for finding himself in jail, and while he says he does hold a union card, that don't mean anything because nearly every man here does. Leva

165

was arrested while paper-hanging in his own home.

Joe Carneghi is a semi-pro ball player.

Pete Hiller is a favorite here, as the youngest man and the only confirmed bachelor. One can see how he could be led by the likes of Otis Clark. Pete was driving his cab when the law caught up to him.

The defense attorney has pointed out the 'slavery' of the nonunion fields in Kentucky and Pennsylvania. He said these men on trial were 'as desperate as a bunch of longhorn Texas cattle lying on the desert sand and fighting off gnats.'

The whole community feels that the union has proved itself as a social and business institution. Their first law is 'keep the union field intact.' Now they are facing a higher law and they don't like it.

The so-called massacre and its trial was the only news and the people's passion. One paper reported that Ignatz Kubens, who'd been shot in the leg by the infamous barbed wire fence, had to have it amputated. Another wrote that the prosecutor had tried to paint a picture of Mrs. Sneed being harangued in her own home by a union mob demanding arms and ammo, even though Mr. Sneed was their elected official twice-over.

The defense countered, "They were half-grown kids. If she'd thrown a soft potato at them they'd have fallen dead. She told those kids that if they wanted the guns they'd have to come in and get them and they melted away."

Ignatz Kubens, shot in his leg by the infamous barbed wire fence, died of complications resulting from amputation. And Commander Hathaway of the Veterans of Foreign Wars, Chicago chapter, asked to be allowed to transport the body of war hero Antonio Malkovaich home, but he stayed where he was in an unmarked mass grave in the warm Herrin cemetery.

And when the trials concluded, all the papers were happy to be able to report—for very different reasons—that not a single person had been convicted of a crime; all were acquitted; all went free.

CHAPTER TWENTY

After a long conversation with Doc House—about fried chicken, cloghoppers, and dirty fried-chicken eating cloghopping morticians—down in the damp basement where Doc made his false teeth, Will went home to Cora. He would be firm but compassionate, and he would change his own ways whether that came up or not. Theirs had been a long marriage and forward was the only reasonable and humane way out. He felt a little tickle of joy at the thought of simplifying his life.

Shelley was sitting with Cora in his kitchen. Both women were smugly triumphant; he saw that at a glance. Cora had said he should help Jeremy Brown because his mother was a good worker who never stole anything important. But now he knew she'd lied by omission, since Shelley had talked to her before that. Being together would amplify their enjoyment of his humiliation.

Shelley rose to leave and cheerily thanked Cora for the tea. Cora didn't answer but not from discourtesy. The look Cora gave him! This was the last thing in the world he was prepared for, and when Shelley was gone Cora loosed her new knowledge on him as casually as somebody had blown off Jordie Henderson's face. She talked and talked about morals and values and ethics, getting the words confused, but he wasn't about to correct her. She got quieter and quieter the longer she spoke until Sneed had to lean toward her to hear, against his best instincts for self-preservation.

But what about you! he shouted when his anger finally took hold, which took them into new realms of accusation and recrimination, prosecution and defense. But in the domestic court there was no judge or jury.

The worst of it came at the end when she admitted to feelings long ago. Since they were finally being open with each other, she said meanly... forget Van Buren, that was nothing whatsoever. It was a double goad for Sneed. He sat in his heavy brick house he'd always thought castle-like, impregnable—at least defensible—and thought of time apart from Cora, all those months, year after year, when he'd traveled for the union. For the first time in his life he felt true regret for something he'd done, and it redoubled when the Van Buren nonsense folded in on him, so he blamed himself for that too, and the harm it would do to his own children, whose faces came to mind in turn. In a flash he remembered his courtship of Cora, winning her over that other boy, and the timing of their marriage scant months before Ruby was born with her dark Italian face. Insensibly he shouted, shook, threatened, and raged, until Cora, sitting taking it, broke and screamed, "I hate you! I hate you! I wish I was dead!" She grabbed a butcher knife from a drawer, walked stiffly past behind him and up the stairs, slammed the bedroom door, and turned the lock savagely. She began to wail in inconsolable grief.

Sneed stood dumbfounded. He was frightened but very very tired at the thought of whatever had to come next. He wondered if it was impossible to resign his offices and move on to something else, anywhere else. He didn't want to slide back down to being a miner but there was a certain freedom in being merely a laborer. Fewer people to deal with. Even a family was a bitter congress.

While the nation raged at the savagery and injustice of all involved in the Southern Illinois massacre going free, Jeremy came dragging home in unshakeable relief. Shelley was mad at him, he knew, but that was understandable. She was religious and hadn't been there that day to see how it all came about. If she had been, she would have seen...well, maybe not. But that didn't mean there wasn't some small right thing in what happened. Jeremy was just happy to be out of the jailhouse. He grinned around her in pleasure and did her chores, enduring her silence until he couldn't take it anymore—it only took two hours—especially since he was doing all her work. He began to pry the lid off just to see what was inside.

"So where we headed? You can see I'm loose now."

"We aren't going anywhere," Shelley said bitterly.

"We'll save up and go. Come on, Shelley. I can make some money building houses. Otis Clark said his brother-in-law would hire me on. When I was in jail...."

He paused, aware he'd made an error. "I was talking to some guys," he began again, hopefully. "They said you can walk up the Eiffel Tower and see all the way across Europe. And there's clubs and music. The food of kings available to everybody. They can show us something about living, I bet."

"Europeans lost the right to such pretensions with their filthy European wars," Shelley snapped. "Bunch of brutes in nice clothes. Why would they dare speak to us at all?"

"Shelley, please. It's okay if you don't want to go anymore. Just don't be mad at me, I can't take it. We'll do whatever you want to, but tell me it's going to be okay. Tell me you still love me."

"I should slap your *head* off," Shelley said. "Some of these crackers live like hogs, they drank their brains out long before the Herrin Massacre, how else would you expect them to act. But Mama raised you to know better and you went and did something this *stupid*. Your sinning aside, I've lost everything because of you including my hope for *your* future. Get out of here and don't come back. You're the worst of them all. I never get to have anything." She wept.

Jim—aka Patrick—O'Rourke left Southern Illinois for the north as soon as Dr. Black would allow him to go, but he left cautiously, more cautiously than he'd ever gone before. The weeks in bed and the long train journey home gave him plenty of time to decide some things. Leo was gone without a trace along with his investments, O'Rourke supposed, and he wasn't surprised really. It was Leo's final lesson to him, a valuable one, but if he ever caught that old fart he'd cut his goddamn throat....

Mercy—dear, solid, handsome Mercy—was reliably staffing her father's store when he went to see her. At the end of two weeks they were engaged. After the wedding, Dad explained the set-up: Jim and Mercy would work the two fabric stores at one generous salary, allowing him to semi-retire, and when Dad was ready, they'd buy both stores from him, lock, stock, and barrel. Jim loved Mercy dearly for the chance she and her old man had given him for a new start. He'd wanted it so long.

This was the path to manhood he'd envisioned during that violence and had enlarged in long contemplation while healing inside and out. He recognized it as his resurrection and as such knew it would require the most radical action. For the rest of his long days (he didn't die until 1992, seventy years after being mauled in Bloody Williamson County) Jim O'Rourke considered it the bravest thing he ever did in his life to lay the keys to that Washington Street fabric store on the counter one morning shortly after he opened up, walk out the back door and *never* look back.

"Look who's back," Sally said when he came in.

See, that's part of it, Bully thought. Sarcasm pretending to be clever, but it's really meant to keep me raw. But why? Why would she do that to me? He saw his son lying on his belly on the rag rug with his head raised to see what was going on and knew he couldn't be without the boy.

He needed something different, quick, to cancel what he'd been thinking or the situation would be intolerable. All that came to mind were Jordie's pleas for help. Bully went to the cupboard, pulled out a little tin and daubed the scrapes on his arms with a salve of lard and coal oil. It stung.

"So where you been?" she asked, too furious to look at him.

"Somewhere I didn't have to watch you in action."

"What?" Sally shrieked and jumped from her chair. The baby cried, and Bully stepped back.

"What did you say to me?" she said.

"I've been around, don't you worry," Bully said. "You're not getting rid of me, I'll tell you that right now. But I couldn't be near you for a while."

She snorted. "Like you never condoned violence. Remember that time right after we met? In that tavern down in the Levee District? Don't get all high and mighty. We did what needed to be done."

"It was a dumb play, Sally, and you know it. Besides, that's not all I'm referring to."

"What are you *referring* to?" Sally was wearing what Bully called her pissy face, a theatrical, adolescent dismissal.

"Jordie Henderson told me some things. Before he died he told me some choice things about you, and it made me sick to hear them. You have no honor, do you? No sense of responsibility. No loyalty."

"What, and you're going to believe Jordie Henderson?" Sally said. "What'd he say?"

Bully squatted next to Robert, cupped the back of the baby's head with his palm and didn't answer.

"Wait a minute," Sally said.

Bully studiously focused on the boy.

"Wait just a goddamned minute," Sally said loudly. "What really happened to Jordie, Bully? What happened that day? Did you do something to him because...."

"I told you and everybody else he got his from the mine," Bully shouted.

"You're going to stand there and lie to me? That's why you've been gone so long, *Oscar*. I know you too well. You got mad like you always do and you hurt Jordie for some dumb lie he was telling you and then you come dragging in here to condemn me for anything *I* might have done?"

Sally stood on her toes and put her nose close to Bully's. "How dare you go against your own kind!" she shrieked. "It's the worst cowardice I know!"

"Shut up!" he roared. "I've had it with you. You think because you tell me to do something, and I don't do it like a good little boy, you can punish me for it too?"

"Oh, don't bother with your little display," Sally said, apparently calm again, turning to fold some clothes. "You're just full of wind. You won't do anything. Don't bother yelling at me. I'm not afraid of you.

"I was wrong," she said. "You wouldn't have the balls to mess with a man like Jordie Henderson."

"And you wouldn't have dared fuck him, either," Bully said, looming over her.

"Not for the reasons you think. Just because I wouldn't screw all over the town I live in, the way you did with that little whore in Eldorado when we were down there. I know all about it, Bully. Don't lie."

"Eh," Bully grunted, swiping his hand in dismissal. "There was never anything to that, I told you a million times. Just because you say something, Sally, doesn't make it true. You are capable of saying or doing anything to make somebody believe your version of things."

"Oh, don't you dare.... What do you mean by that?" Sally said, visibly hot again.

"I don't know."

"No, go ahead and say it. You've been thinking it, I know you have."

"Thinking what?"

"You know what. Be a man, get it out there."

"What?" Bully sat down, signaling his refusal to play.

"It's Jacob, isn't it?"

"What about Jacob?" Bully wouldn't look at Sally.

"You think I was to blame for Jacob's death."

Bully was red in the face. "All I know is, he was crying, and I left him with you for one minute, and when I came back he was completely still. He died in your hands," Bully cried, panting now.

"You evil son-of-a-bitch," Sally said. "You're the one. You're the one with all the suspicions he wasn't yours, and you mistreated him before I ever got home. You killed my baby," she sobbed. "Oh God, Bully, how could you?"

"Not me, *you*! *You* killed my son with your hot goddamned temper and selfishness!" Bully roared.

Sally ran at him, and though Bully had been expecting it, all he could do was raise one leg as she came in. She fell back with his foot in her belly, but when he stood up and leaned over her with his fists to make sure she stayed down, she caught him in the crotch. In the terror of feeling beaten, he punched her in a breast, and though both were already in agony they clawed and kneed each other to exhaustion as their baby screamed on the floor and the neighbors retreated in fear.

In the end, it was impossible to say who got the worst of it, a phrase we might well apply to this whole business.

172

CHAPTER TWENTY-ONE

The Rotary was the pre-eminent service club in Herrin, and there was a general feeling in the town that if anyone could smooth over all the difficulties of the last few weeks, from the nightmare of national perception to the rampant rise of bootlegging and violence that sprang up in the wake of the other lawlessness, it was these men, the elite of the community, who with gravity and forethought would reunite and lead the way to better times. Most of them owned businesses in town—the bank, clothing stores, restaurants, the lumberyard, and the new Dodge Brothers automobile dealership—but Dr. Black was there too, as was the mayor, the owner of the *Herrin News*, and the man who ran the paper the next town over. Sneed had cleared time in his schedule and brought with him two sub-district officials who had not been indicted. It was the largest gathering in their chapter's history, excepting barbecues and dances, and a spirit of eager cooperation ruled as each member wondered who in their bunch had murdered, who had allowed it, who was a coward, and what that meant in this case.

"Did you hear about those Herrin boys arrested in Cincinnati for carrying pistols?" Mayor MacCormack asked. "Lamb and Hamby, they're both in their twenties. They made a splash over there. Lamb told that judge, 'We're from Herrin, and we're not ashamed of it. It might have a black eye with the rest of the world, but it is home sweet home and God's country to us.'"

"'Do you walk around in Herrin with murderous-looking revolvers strapped to your waists?' the judge asked."

"'No sir,' Lamb said. 'Herrin is a peaceful little town.'"

The mayor said, "I'm proud of that Lamb boy. I thought he'd turn out no good."

"I apologize," Sneed said. "But I'll have to leave early today, and I just had one bit of news I wanted to share. Lester's mine has been bought by the Caloric Coal Company. It's a new venture with Chicago and Indianapolis capital. Lester sold the mine for one dollar plus considerations, and Burlington took back their rolling stock."

"One dollar?" the bank owner asked. "Considerations?"

"You make money off the death of those men, Will?"

"I won't even dignify that."

"Yes, that's out of line, Pete."

"But I don't suppose any of the considerations were for the union," Trovillion said dryly.

"I wouldn't want to characterize it that way."

"I'm sure you wouldn't," a man mumbled.

"Listen, if anything does come our way it'll be used to help the widows and orphans in this county," Sneed said. "It would be welcome, we need the funds. The sale is all above board."

"Like the deal you had with Lester that let him load coal in the first place?" asked a shopkeeper.

"Sounds like blood money," another said. "Kickbacks."

"That's a bunch of rot spread by the state chamber of commerce," Sneed said. "We've been through all that. Let's move on."

"Yes, Bill's right," the mayor said. "What we must do today is to figure out how to change the tenor of this community. Things have been hard lately, they been hard for a long while, but we have resources and just need to use them for everybody's good."

"Far as all this lawlessness goes," a Rotarian said, "I think we'd best clean it up."

Others defined the issues:

"Whoring."

"Gambling."

"Boozing."

"Gangsters slugging it out in the streets."

"I saw a colored boy looking at Mrs. Triplett's daughter yesterday."

"Well none of that even needs saying," the mayor said. "But how's it get done?"

The august body sat in the August heat and pondered. Those who'd come with agenda pretended to think but were waiting for a natural-seeming moment to present their plans.

"Vigilantes," said one finally, beating out the others.

"No, no, *hell* no. Revert back to the days of Regulators and Red Buttons and all that? Don't be ridiculous."

"Why doesn't the *town* clean things up then? It's your responsibility, Mac."

"You want to hire me a police force five times bigger than I got?" whined the mayor. "Who's gonna vote in the taxes to pay for it?"

"I heard of a former federal lawman that heads up this kind of cleanup," a man said. "Did some real good work out in the Blue Ridge. If we got private funds, the town wouldn't even have to be involved."

"More force won't correct what violence has brought," Hal Trovillion said. "I read recently of an evangelical preacher that worked wonders on towns worse than ours. Let me write to him and see if he'll hold a revival, and we'll bring God back to Herrin."

"We just need to change our image, is all," said the owner and editor of the *Zeigler News*. "Get some other kinds of business and activities in here, so we aren't thought of in terms of coal. Let's face it, that's one ugly rock, and digging it up is a dirty business. Now, a number of people have been telling me health resorts are popular, and they don't take much to start up. Let's turn this whole area into a big spa. We'll bring the rich in from all over, maybe as far as Indianapolis."

The others looked at him.

"Bill, could you arrange for us to meet that federal lawman?" the lumberyard owner and Sneed's sometime bridge partner asked.

"Can we all agree that asking some questions won't do any harm?"

"I don't like what I've heard about this sort of thing," Trovillion said. "Wasn't this fella one of the mine guards for Lester?"

Sneed frowned and looked around for confirmation.

"No, no," a man assured. "That was somebody else. This gent's okay."

"Some of these men get their wind up and take it out on us Catholics, you know," said a Rotarian.

"They get rough with the bootleggers."

"But that's the point, Tommy."

"Is it?"

"Excuse me," Sneed said, rising to go. "I'm late for another meeting.

Why don't I just track this man down through my contacts in Washington, and if he is what he says he is, we can meet with him to consider it. No harm in that, right?"

Most of the Rotarians nodded, and the group thanked Sneed as he left. They stuck around to hash out other ideas for revitalizing the local economy, assuming the lawlessness could be curbed, but there weren't many viable proposals.

The next week the Rotarians read the Zeigler paper with annoyance:

> Few people realize this city is making a record as a health resort equaled by few cities of its size. According to reports reaching the Zeigler News, there has been only two deaths within the past eighty days. One of these was caused by a shooting following the love of two men for one woman, leaving only one death from sickness and this just an infant. There are few cities of over 5,000 population that can boast of this record. We have the flower of manhood and womanhood in this part of the state.
>
> The city administration assisted by Zeigler News organized the annual cleanup day which has met with hearty cooperation on the part of the public. Rubbish and tin cans have been removed from the city. The breeding places of flies and filth have been destroyed and causes for disease have been removed. While the city needs considerable more cleaning up to be the sort of health resort that will draw people from all parts of the world, the condition is much better than it was a short time ago, and it will only get better and better. The rest of the county has agreed to think about following our lead.

CHAPTER TWENTY-TWO

How alone we are together, Sneed thought, as he dropped the kids and Cora on the steps of the First Baptist with the other churchgoers filing in through the doors. In the year since the Lester incident, public piety had risen in equal measure to violence, and merchants all over town had signs in their windows that read, "THIS PLACE WILL BE CLOSED AT NOON FOR PRAYER." If they wanted to advertise their true nature, they should wear letters on their starched Sunday shirts instead, he thought: K for killer. He'd dreaded church all week but parked the car and took his seat in his family's pew as the choir sang "Free From the Law, O Happy Condition":

Now we are free—
There's no condemnation,
Jesus provides
A perfect salvation.
"Come unto Me,"
Oh, hear his sweet call,
Come, and He saves us
Once for all.

Reverend Lee gave the opening prayer then Don Childers stood to testify. He looked nervous as he approached the lectern and pulled at his pants where the pistol in his pocket was bothering him. Lee gave him the nod.

"Last Tuesday I was in my house," Childers said shakily. "I got dizzy and very thirsty and a voice spoke to me. It said: Go to your church."

"Judgment will start in the house of the Lord!" a man in the audience called in encouragement.

"The voice said, Go tell your sins to your brothers and sisters down to the Baptist Church. Tell them, *tell* them what it is you done!" Childers began to sob quietly.

"We love you, Brother! Praise the Lord!"

Let's have it, Sneed thought angrily.

"I dress too well," Childers said. "It's true. I'm prideful, the sin of sins. You can see it here today. Look at these two-toned shoes I bought over at the Jew's clothing store last week on sale. He talked me into a bowler hat too, I was so weak."

"Hell was *created* for the father of lies!" a woman cried.

"Also, Tuesday last I had a drink that made me take the Lord's name." Childers warmed to the performance and tears streamed down his face.

Sweat broke out on Sneed's upper lip, and he shifted in his seat, very near panic. Sure, Childers was bawling now but he'd be balling his secretary in the Herrin Motel come Monday noon. Great day in the morning, what rot. No one ever got up to atone for much, though there was that one marvelous Sunday when Marta Doederlein stood and admitted to selling her body for lucre and began the roll call of all those who'd had her. Men were sliding off the pews and crawling out the door *that* morning.

Childers eventually turned from his own woes to help his fellows. "We will *all* stand for judgment," he wailed. "Sin is a barrier that keeps us from reaching God. It starts from small and increases and increases. And there's only one antidote for sin!"

"Amen!"

He was fluent now. "I am a salesman of Christ and a salesman must know his goods!"

"Thank you, Brother, that was magnificent," Pastor Lee said, frowning as if Childers meant to horn in on his business, and guided him offstage by an elbow.

"I ain't done!" Childers said.

Sneed knew it was his own fault. He'd trapped *himself* in a system of family, career, union, and community that had been built intricately and painstakingly over years and years of his life, and now the system demanded his attendance at this church this morning. He was no longer free to omit one part he hated; it would be like omitting nails from a house. A man might choose which system he wanted to help build, but once built it became his fate. He knew everyone here and they knew him, neighbors couldn't be any closer, especially given what they'd been through together the last year, but he had a little epiphany that made him shiver in the heat: Maybe he had no people and never would. Maybe this grim loneliness was real manhood, at which youth only pretended.

He'd seen Shelley only twice after he promised Cora he wouldn't. It would have been better if he'd done as promised. He and Shelley were awkward and regretful with each other, and Jeremy had been there both times, acting sullen and grown-up. He'd started in as a hod carrier for another of the men indicted in the Lester affair, and Shelley deferred to him. He said Shelley was going to start in on their mother's line of work.

Sally and Bully had moved down to Saline County to some place called Pankeyville. She was pregnant again, and everybody gossiped she was too old to carry a baby full-term but it probably didn't matter anyway given how *those* two got along. There were stories about the death of their other child.

There were also stories floating around that he or Cora had said the word divorce.

"Morality is like a coal mine," Reverend Lee intoned at the start of his sermon.

Jesus, not this old saw, Sneed thought. Who's he think he is, Father Taylor of Boston?

"We try our best to brattice off the rooms of our sin. We may manage to do so for a time, even for decades, but those sins always threaten to blow us up," he said. "If we know what's good for us, we vent those rooms and rid them of their miasmas."

No, Sneed thought, usually we pump in water and sulfur to drown the memories. Then we cover the past over with bullshit and grow jokes on top. But the very ground under our feet is riddled with those wormholes, and sometimes entire houses fall into them.

"For the past year-and-a-half no little city on the American continent has been so much in the international news as Herrin. People all over God's green Earth are asking, What manner of city is it that so frequently disturbs the nation with its outlandish deportment? Those who dwell afar pose hard questions about the sort of people we are and how it all

179

came to this.

"Something spreads from violence like ripples from a dunked stone, and it widens, weakens, and comes back on itself in waves. This county has been lawless for a hundred years, going back to the feuds, the vendettas, and the secessionist movement. Now we wonder how to go forward, how we're to be forgiven our past, and the answer lies only in the blood of the Lamb. Blessed are the peacemakers, those who long for righteousness, those whose hearts are pure. So saith the Lord."

Sneed suspected Lee was speaking to him. He knew he still had the strength to be a peacemaker, if that was to be his role, but it was no longer an enthusiasm he felt in his body. He'd had to dance for the House Committee investigation on the Lester incident. Pierce, the chairman, had treated him as a hostile witness. Then he helped bury the senate report too so it hadn't been a news event. He *would* work even harder in future, and campaign for re-election on the basis of having done that work, but at heart he felt his efforts were dross. The town was a wilderness of hate; everyone acted as if they were mad.

Reverend Lee continued. "Herrin is America writ small. Never mind we have Italians, families from North England and Wales, Lithuanians, Polanders, and even a few Syrians, or that in the war's aftermath a lot of idle men from Alabama and the West Kentucky coalfields were attracted to our community. The great mass of us are Pure Americans. Yet with all that unaccountable rash action out to the Lester place, we're seen as everything Americans don't like to claim."

Sneed's thoughts slipped away. He got his best thinking done in church and during band concerts. It was one of the glories of a society, sharing an event you all ignored together.

It had been his young man's dream to think something big could be accomplished in a short period, if only enough energy could be summoned. A much different energy would be needed to chip away at the tricky and complicated tasks of the next twenty-five or thirty years of his working life, and he felt himself become no longer young in that moment, as if something fluid in him suddenly found its catalyst, and he'd become crystalline, brittle. Perhaps it was for the best. He'd been bothered with idealism too long—another mark against innate political genius.

It was time to do what must be done, and to do it coldly and surely.

Organized labor was in a mess, and their district was symptomatic of the problem. Sally and her Socialist, Wobbly, and Communist friends were bitterly against compromise, and he was sure they'd try to smear him eventually by saying he'd sold them out. They refused to accept that machines would soon let owners mine twice the tonnage with half the men, and that holding out against them would only delay the inevitable. John Lewis had hinted at bringing Sneed on to help forge a new way with capital. Sally and the others could go right ahead and splinter off. Maybe they'd take the immigrant ranks with them. Sneed intended to create work for the others. His attention floated back to the sermon.

"Our *felix culpa*, our fortunate fall, was bigger and better than the city of Chicago's great conflagration," the pastor was saying.

"No, ours was a *moral* fall, not some mere natural disaster brought on by the cloven-hooved. We were the agents of our own destruction and now are free to choose salvation. The sinful ruins left this community are still too smoking-hot for outsiders to handle. But not for us—it's our trade, our lives.

"Maybe the coal industry is finished. That seems impossible, but you've heard those who say it's so. If it is, fine then: We'll bring industry here. We'll expand our farms. With our resources, our will, and just a little of God's good providence, we will succeed. 'In Him, all things hold together.' This community, which the rest of America has shunned, will be a brotherhood just as the lodges and other societies teach and try to practice."

Sneed had been a Freemason since those early awkward days, and he began to feel the stir of the call.

"But who will lead us in this?" Lee begged, looking up at Sneed. "It need not be a job for a martyr, just someone with the *will* to show the way. We *will* need men big enough, brave enough, cunning enough for the job, who *will* model the nerve, power, and love of the true and faithful servant of Christ. We need men who can turn lemons thrown at them into a cool, sweet, smiling drink, men who can catch, seed, and juice them as fast as they're pitched. *They will* be the ones to take the guns out of hip pockets and put in their place clean handkerchiefs. The whole fabric of government is woven upon the practice of true Christian civilization."

In his peripheral vision Sneed saw Cora reach her hand out to him with the palm up and open. Her eyes were closed. He was astonished that she too had heard in Lee's words his call to renewed service, and he was joyous. Only Cora's opinion of him mattered, only her forgiveness would do. He slid his hand onto hers and clasped fingers with her, the damp heat of her skin an ecstasy. He looked to the stained-glass window of Golgotha, a red glass sun rising behind the hill, the real sun outside blazing through in congruence, and felt he might cry with pleasure that there was hope and love in this congregation after all, and the urge to make something good.

Sneed's youngest, two-year old Helen, looked up in adoration as if she knew his heart. Civilization was the power of women. He knew it was prideful—funny old Childers—to see himself reflected in his toddler's eyes, but he didn't withhold the pleasure of drafting what she'd say one day as a grown woman when he lay cold on the bier at the front of this assembly:

Daddy was truly one of God's men. He was an example to his country, community, and family and a beloved friend among the different economic classes, religious denominations, nationalities, and races. His warm handclasp, hearty laugh, and dynamic personality opened all doors for his immeasurable success.

As if on cue, the church doors flew open like wings, revealing the glare and heat of the day, and seven hooded knights of the Ku Klux Klan marched up the aisle toward the pulpit. It was their first showing in the area, though they were well-known in Ohio, and they arrayed themselves to face the congregation in a way both showy and threatening. Their leader stepped over and handed an envelope to Reverend Lee, who opened it and fanned the dollars inside like a hand of cards, his face a mask of O! delight. There was also a short note inside on Christian unity, which he read aloud once they'd filed out again.

In the deathly silence that followed their departure, Sneed shouted with something like laughter, and when we turned to look at him we nearly said, Didn't you put us in touch with that avowed lawman?, but we saw in his eyes that he already knew that by being who he was and living as he'd hoped to become, he was inextricably and eternally sunk in Little Egypt.

Epilogue

this heart eternal blew to pieces rejoined in helices so mother was matter in points as far from god as most are truth and

froze and bulged time after again, smoothed in great grinding slabs that moved us in our moving. felt to stopping in the wink of billennium and so did. shrank from moraines of rock flour and splintered trees, poured downcontinent, dug downvalley thousands long, never tiring of watery tricks—liquid, gas, solid—shifting shapes at every chance, alluvial silt and sand spreading, settling in striated clays and shales—a real messy geomorphology. and

Coral-gathered our deaths in limestone castles and grinned round them in brute perfection. Dark early waters home to cockles that echoed waves, eternal music for happyselves, the harps of trilobites frozen in bluffs. Fell saltwater through heaven to become fresh. Cast splash in sandstone to read the notes and see rain rhythm always. And

We watched with dusty black eyes as the grasses thrived and wilted and sank into bogs, and grew and wilted and died, and strained and wilted, and sediment washed over the peat in quick waves longer than the ages. Shale and crude were trapped under our thin skin, and we shifted in our beds until rock thrust up in unsubtle randy forms. Our home is the crotch between the rivers. And.

We sprouted as okra and rhubarb by way of attempting human shape. So too the brainy walnut, the fuzzed flesh of peaches, sweet reeking mounds of honeysuckle. Pumpkins got guts. The cucumber had form and seed like the phallus but needed no body; it was perfect in its play. Boulders grimaced in profile on the sky; persimmons blushed; willows wept; when we were violets we were as shrinking as spinsters. All this took time, and we looked upon our single body and its many shapes in happy wonder.

And cell by living cell we became bluegill, because it felt good to splash in pond's warm bath. Lapped at river's edge, shivered at wind-ruffled faces. Became bear, because bluegill and blackberries were so delicious. Through imagination all these things were done.

We stampeded game off cliffs and feasted on their bones for fifteen thousand years. Built man's greatest earthworks to praise the shapes of deity, grew holy corn and traded geodes for oyster shells. Our villages rose and fell and we moved on one another and killed in living. Then along came the white man, drove the bison out. Down came the plagues. They marched our sons away. Dirty furbeadtraders shafted us again.

And let me tell you what: We were some tree-choppin', prairie-breakin', land-tamin', buffalo-huntin', squirrel-eatin', bare-knuckle fightin' snazzy dressers and fancy dancers.

Then, where one hundred men and women once lived as smiths, lacemakers, potters, coopers, wrights and farmers, now ten thousand thrived in wasps' nests of brick, and what they saw when they looked back at us were screwy little dopes who whistled while we worked. That many worked harder than ever in the dark and wet for the few to make their nights electric was not the point. We began to grow wistful that there had been days when *We* was true.

We hacked at the earth with machines that chewed the rock and spit it into foundries that cast bigger digging machines, thinking only briefly that if we left the coal alone it might become diamonds one day, inexpressible riches for our children's children's children. But we couldn't wait for that, and they told us scientifically that our fields would not be exhausted until the year 2714. They came back two years later and said it's over.

We're down here with hundreds of years of fuel just waiting to flame to life. There's veins of rich black coal under here twenty feet thick, millions of tons, even if you have to dig down a thousand feet to get it. We've never lost faith. We have everything. We have water, and we have land to hold the water. And we have fuel and crops and family and hope.

We *will* you, our kin, this earth to dig, to haul, to break, to burn. Consign yourself to the flames in which we meet and come to know. This is your inheritance: conflagration in the fire buried in all our atomic forms. We speak of coal and slate; algae, songbirds and kings; curious lives that burn in the cycles to leave only clinkers, slag, and ash. But the flames themselves are inexhaustible, and we vessels are fire-formed time and again to contain, deliver, and serve. *We....*

ACKNOWLEDGMENTS

Letter excerpts courtesy of University of Illinois Library, Illinois Historical Survey, John Hunter Walker Collection.

Selected material paraphrased from *People of Coal Town*. Herman R. Lantz. New York: Columbia University Press, 1958.

Reverend Lee's sermon adapted from *Persuading God Back to Herrin*. Hal Trovillion, Editor, *The Herrin News*. Herrin, Illinois: 1925.

Background and context for the Herrin Massacre and other violent episodes in Southern Illinois history can be found in *Bloody Williamson: A Chapter in American Lawlessness*, the best nonfiction book on the subject. Paul M. Angle. Champaign: University of Illinois Press, 1993.

"The props assist the house" by Emily Dickinson reprinted by permission of the publishers and the Trustees of Amherst College from *The Poems of Emily Dickinson*, Thomas H. Johnson, ed., Cambridge, Mass.: The Belknap Press of Harvard University Press, Copyright © 1951, 1955, 1979, 1983 by the President and Fellows of Harvard College.

Excerpt of Phillip Kinsley's article of November 18, 1922 (pg. 165), used with permission of the *Chicago Tribune*; copyright *Chicago Tribune*, all rights reserved.

Thanks to John Hoffmann, Illinois History and Lincoln Collections, University of Illinois Library; the staff of the Chicago History Museum Research Center; the staff of Morris Library, Southern Illinois University Carbondale; Cornell University's School of Industrial and Labor Relations; and Peter Berg, Special Collections, Michigan State University Libraries.

Thanks to Steve Davenport, who got it rolling, and to Duff Brenna, my editor. I am also grateful to have been read by Gary DeNeal, Herb Russell, Gordon Pruett, Mike Finke, Priscilla Long, and Caroline Merithew. Thanks to Charlie S. Jensen, Jim Leveille, John T. Dempsey, Melanie Hobson, Jim Ballowe, Doug Lederman, Peter Mortensen, and John Warner for their support and friendship. Most of all, thanks to my family: the Sneeds, Griswolds, Bruces, Luckeys, and Eisenhauers.

ABOUT THE AUTHOR

John Griswold lives with his wife and sons in Urbana, Illinois, where he teaches at the University of Illinois.

His writing has appeared in *Ninth Letter, Brevity*, and *Natural Bridge*, which nominated him for the Pushcart Prize, and in the anthologies *The Best Creative Nonfiction, Vol. 3* (W.W. Norton) and *Mountain Man Dance Moves* (McSweeney's Books). His single-story chapbook, *The Stork*, is available from Featherproof Books. He's currently at work on a nonfiction book about Herrin, Illinois, which will be published in 2010 by The History Press.

John has also written extensively under the pen name Oronte Churm. As Churm he is a contributing writer for *Inside Higher Ed* and a columnist for *McSweeney's*.

Read more at JohnGriswold.net.

for other Wordcraft of Oregon titles
please visit our website at
www.wordcraftoforegon.com

Printed in the United States
152029LV00003B/248/P

9 781877 655630